The Other Man

Published February 2016.

Please note:

'The Other Man' is a work of fiction. Any and all names, characters, places and/or events described in this book are works of fiction. Any similarity between this and real persons, living or dead, events, establishments or location are purely coincidental and not intended by the author. Please do not take offense to the content included as it is fiction.

This book also identifies product/object names and services known to be registered trademarks or service marks of their respective holders. The author acknowledges the trademark status in this work of fiction but the publication of said trademarks is not authorised, associated with or sponsored by the trademark owners.

AUTHOR NOTE

Because talking is my thing...

Well, it's done.

This book has been in the works for over a year but I couldn't find the right words to finish it. Obviously, this is just book one and there is so much more to come but the content and storyline were difficult for me. I pushed myself so far out of my comfort zone with this.

For any of you who have read my previous books, you should know that I usually try and combine a clear love story with smut and touch of humour.

This book is different.

The emotions, the angst...the sexual frustration, that I felt when I was writing Blake's story was off the charts!

My guy makes mistakes and I'm sure he'll make a few of you angry but please forgive him because I promise you he's not a bad guy. I like to think that his story is truly unique and that you won't be able to prevent yourself from being sucked into his life.

I didn't want to write a warning with the synopsis. I think it should speak for itself. I think my personality in general usually makes people blush, but this pushes those boundaries even further.

However, you've bought it now, so there's no turning back! *Evil laugh*

My books are like my babies and the unwritten rules state that I can't choose a favourite. I've never been a fan of rules and I broke that one when I'd written the first chapter of The Other Man.
The characters and the storyline, they both hold a special place in my heart. I have never been so excited, or nervous, to hit publish.

Prepare to be annoyed, frustrated, angry...and turned on beyond all measures ;-)
I hope you enjoy reading this book half as much as I enjoyed writing it.

PROLOGUE
In the beginning...

I, Blake James Thomas, take you, Carlie Marie Locke, to have and to hold, for better for worse, for richer for poorer, in sickness and in health, to love and to cherish from this day forward.

Until death do us part.

Traditional wedding vows.

When you're head over heels in love with someone, you truly believe every vow you make is forever. You promise to spend your entire life with that person. Make them happy every day, make them smile, laugh. Be the person they can rely on, the person who is always there for them.

The person they can *trust.*

As much as it pains me to admit it, that's just not always the case.

Considering the divorce rate in the UK is more than thirty-nine percent, I guess other people would have to agree with me.

A marriage doesn't have to mean forever anymore, as sad as that is, it's true. It takes work, effort, compromise...and even then, it just might not be enough.

Want to know why I think that is?

Soulmates.

Ok, so you might disagree with me, but just for a second, put yourself in this situation. Whether you've been married for three weeks or thirty years, you could be blissfully happy, have children, holiday homes and a beautiful life.

Then you meet your soulmate.

He's the guy working behind the bar, or the new postman, or your boss. As 'in love' as you are, there's just something about him. He makes your heart race, your stomach flutter and your mind starts to drift. What would it feel like to kiss him? To hold him?

I know what you're thinking, you don't have to act on it. You love your husband and you'd never cheat on him. Ok, so say you didn't cheat, the thoughts are still there. You'll start to doubt things that you'd never even thought about before. That adorable way your husband scowls at the TV, the way he sighs when you won't let him get a word in edgeways, the way he clicks his nails together when he's getting impatient. Tiny little actions will start to annoy you, you'll snap at him more, he'll get frustrated.

You'll argue.

The doubts will get worse.

It wasn't always like this, was it?

Do I still love him? Was I ever *really* in love with him?

It's an endless cycle and it can kill a marriage easily.

Wait, wait, I'm not saying this happens to everyone, because it doesn't.

Maybe you're one of the lucky ones who actually married their soulmate, or maybe you'll never meet yours.

...Maybe I'm just judgemental and cynical. Who knows?

But life happens.

And life happened to me in a *huge* way.

I've made mistakes, *monumental* mistakes. I've hurt myself, hurt others. I've been lost and confused, angry and devastated.

But I don't regret a single thing.

Life can be tough sometimes and not everything works out the way you expect, or even the way you wanted it to.

Weather the storm. Fight it, brand it, and make life *your* bitch.

Because it's worth it in the end.

...and here's my story.

I warn you, it's not pretty and you'll probably dislike me *a lot*. So be it. I'm ok with that because everything happens for a reason.

Even if that *reason*, is a person.

CHAPTER
One

February 2005 - Ten years before

Have you ever had one of those moments in your life where you stop and think, 'life really doesn't get much better than this?'

I was in that moment.

I gazed down at Carlie. Her long, blonde hair pulled high, curled, styled and beautiful. I couldn't wait to get my hands on it, in it, and let it hang down around her shoulders. The way she usually wore it, the way I liked it.

In her tight, fitted but flowing, pristine white dress, she looked every inch the princess that she was. Flawless figure, flawless face, flawless hair. She looked incredible.

Perfectly put-together.

My Carlie did not let herself look any less than perfect, that much was true. This, however, just made me want to throw her down on the nearest surface, tear her dress and fuck her until she couldn't walk. Granted, any time she was near me, I wanted to do that. I just wanted to mess her up a bit and make her look like she belonged to me.

Regardless, she actually *was* mine. Officially.

As of a few minutes before, the vicar had

declared us husband and wife.

Carlie. Mine.

For every minute, of every day, for the rest of our lives.

Six months. She'd had six months to plan our wedding down to the very last detail. And when I say every detail, I meant it. The flower petals that ran along the aisle matched the shade of the decorations, matched the shade of the bridesmaids dresses, which matched the ribbons on the wedding cars, my tie, the ushers handkerchiefs...the list went on and on.

She wanted her perfect wedding, and considering her dad was covering the entire cost, who was I to argue?

It was done, she was mine, and we were about to fly off for two weeks in the sun for our honeymoon. The trip was the one thing I put my foot down on. Her dad was *not* paying for it, even though I had to scrimp and save for months. I knew it would be worth it.

After sparing a few minutes so she could change out of her wedding dress, Carlie was ready and as the plane sped along the runway, I reached over and took her fingers between mine, admiring our rings side-by-side.

A single day, a ring of metal, a few spoken words in front of a church full of people and I was a married man. It seemed so simple, almost too easy, to sign my commitment to one person for the rest of my life.

Where were the classes?

Where was the training?

Surely we, as mere human beings, needed some kind of guidance when we're making promises to each other that are supposed to last forever.

My palms started to sweat as the plane's front

wheels lifted from the tarmac and I had that momentary feeling of weightlessness, Carlie's eyes were on me.

"You're nervous," she noted incorrectly.

I was not nervous, I was in full blown panic mode.

And my panic was neither to do with the take-off of the plane, or the flight that was commencing. No, my panic was born from the fact that I was getting a severe case of cold-feet...*after* I was already married. Where were my doubts beforehand?

Carlie's fingers squeezed around mine, anchoring me to the present.

"Don't be nervous, baby. I've got you."

She did. She had me. My lungs filled and I breathed easier. My Carlie. My beautiful wife. She had me and she always would.

The flight dragged on and nine hours later, we landed, exiting into the blistering heat of the sun beating down on Havana International Airport. I'd chosen Cuba for our honeymoon for one reason only. That reason being that when I'd seen the pictures of the villa online and the private pool it boasted, I could already picture Carlie's naked skin as she worked on her tan. I could picture her lying on her front, arms crossed above her head, legs slightly apart, pert, round ass on display.

And there wasn't another villa within walking distance.

Total, complete seclusion.

I could fuck her out there. I could oil her up, slide my fingers inside her pussy, bring her to the brink and then slam home. Make her moan my name, make her scream and no one was close enough to hear a thing. It was a fantasy I'd had more than once since I'd booked and paid for the holiday and I was about forty minutes away from making that fantasy my reality.

My timeline didn't quite work out the way I wanted it to.

Getting through passport control, customs and retrieving our cases seemed easy compared to my attempts at getting the keys for our rental car. The extremely polite, extremely helpful older lady at the desk...spoke Spanish.

Only Spanish.

This would have been just fine, providing either me or Carlie could speak a word of the language and we couldn't. In hindsight, yes, it would have been a great idea to learn the basic of the main language for the country we were staying in. In my defence, I had been told that the majority of residents and *all* of the people who worked with tourists in any capacity, spoke English. It didn't bode well for us that the third person we'd come into contact with, didn't.

We spent almost an hour going back and forth with the woman, trying to explain that we just needed the keys to our rental, and directions to where to pick it up. We were annoyed, she was annoyed, and it didn't bode well.

I held up my keys from home and wiggled them.

"Keys," I said slowly. Then pointed to a taxi parked outside. "Car? We need keys to our car."

"Lo siento, no puedo entenderte," she replied, sounding apologetic. "Mi colega habla inglés, él regresará pronto. Sí?"*

She may as well have been speaking gorgon for all I could understand. Growling in frustration, I looked around for anyone that might be able to help us out. Then Carlie, who had been furiously fingering the pages of the translation dictionary she'd rushed over to buy from the airport store, squeaked.

"I think I did it!" She shoved a scrap of paper towards the woman. "Gracias, Entiendes?"**

My jaw dropped and I made a decision that the second we got home from the holiday, she needed to take Spanish lessons. The way those two single words rolled of her tongue, the sound of her voice, I wanted more of it. She spoke again, still in Spanish.

"Mi nombre es Carlie, ¿y tú?"***

The woman behind the desk closed her eyes in relief, then they opened again and she spoke rapidly, "Oh gracias a Dios! Mi nombre es Catrina. Te ruego que me diga lo que usted necesita. Si ya tienes un coche reservado, necesito tu nombre, el depósito y la prueba de identificación."****

Carlie's went wide. Too much, too fast.

In a flurry, a tall, skinny guy came bustling through the backdoor of the little wooden shack and he immediately began speaking. In English. Thank fuck.

"Sorry, so sorry! Traffic, you know?"

I blinked, "No, I don't know because I don't have a fucking car yet!"

"Blake," Carlie scolded, hooking her hold into the crook of my elbow. She spoke to the new guy. "Sorry about him, it's been a long couple of days and we're exhausted. We just need to pick up the keys to our rental and get directions to where we have to go and collect it."

In exactly three minutes, we had the keys, the paperwork, a map, and I was climbing into the driver's seat of the 4x4 we'd rented for the fortnight.

I looked at Carlie, she looked over at me and grinned, "No puedo esperar para hacer el amor con mi esposo."*****

"I have no idea what you said but whatever it was, makes me want to stick my dick in you!"

She giggled and pulled her knees up to her chest, "Maybe one day, I'll tell you."

The rest of the journey to the villa flew by with no issues. I noticed our little honeymoon hideaway before she did and it looked every bit as perfect as the pictures. Pure luxury. I indicated and turned the car into the driveway.

I knew exactly when Carlie had realised that we had arrived because she gasped in shock, "Tell me that's not ours."

"For two weeks, darling, this is ours," I confirmed.

She squealed, "Oh my god, Blake! This is amazing!"

She was right, it really was amazing. Clean, gleaming white tiles glistened in the sunlight, illuminating the walls of the villa, giving it the image of an ethereal vision.

"It looks like a palace," Carlie whispered, voice tinged with wonder.

"It's small, but it's perfect for us. I wanted this holiday to be perfect for *you*, darling."

She dived out of the vehicle as soon as I pulled the handbrake and she ran towards the pool, "Look at it, Blake! I can't even, I don't know how to," She paused and looked back at me. "Thank you. I love you, honey, so much. Can you grab one of the cameras from my bag for me? I want to make sure I take tons of photos to show everyone back home what you did for me!"

I grabbed one of the cameras and threw it over to her, leaning against the car to watch her. Her excitement radiated from her and seeped into my skin. If my mission was to make her happy, and it was, then I was already succeeding.

I figured that the whole 'husband' thing couldn't be that difficult, I'd just learn along the way.

That job was made a little more difficult due to the fact that Carlie was a daddy's girl. Spoilt, bratty, demanding. But sweet, generous and cute too so it didn't faze me. I was her protector, her husband and it was my job to give her the world and everything in it.

"Honey, do you mind if I jump straight in the pool? I can't wait! Will you be ok bringing our things in by yourself?"

Rolling my eyes, I told her I'd be fine and to go ahead. I dragged our two cases (I only had half of one) into the villa, and returned to the car to bring in all the extra pieces. With everything thrown around the lounge and dining area, I put my hands in the pockets of my shorts, took a good fifteen minutes to survey the inside of our little temporary home and my lips tipped up. Yeah, I'd done well.

I paused.

Carlie went in the pool.

Our luggage was inside, meaning Carlie didn't have anything to wear in the pool.

I kicked off my shoes, grabbed a bottle of suntan oil and jogged to the patio doors, opening them wide and stepping outside. I struggled to breathe.

Carlie lay stretched out on her front, on a lounger. Her arms crossed above her head, her legs slightly parted and her pert, round ass was calling to me.

But it was better.

Because she'd been in the pool.

Little rivers of water dripped from the ends of her hair and ran down her back to the top of her ass.

Beads of it dotted around her skin made her glisten in the sunlight and my cock sprang to life behind my shorts. I put my hands into my waistband and slid the shorts down, careful not to make a sound. My bare feet were silent as I creeped across the patio until I stood, my shins to her feet, blocking the sun from Carlie's body.

She attempted to turn over but I put my palm in between her shoulders and pushed her back down.

"Blake, honey, you're blocking my sun."

My voice thick with passion, I watched her body tense as it rumbled through her.

"Don't move," I held the bottle of oil upside down over her back and let streams of liquid fall onto her skin. "Would be a waste if all this flawless skin got burned on the first day, don't you think?"

I put oil into one hand and rubbed both together. Starting at her ankles, I smoothed my palms along the silkiness of her calves, squeezing and moulding her flesh, massaging the oil into her skin. I reached the apex of her thighs and they quivered in anticipation, so I moved and started again at the base of her back.

She moaned in frustration and I bit my lip to hide my grin.

Inching higher, I moved to her spine, her shoulders and her neck. Her skin shone, she was writhing and whimpering. I still hadn't even touched her where she really wanted me to.

"Blake..." she begged.

I slapped her ass. She yelped, "What was that for?"

"You'll get me, you know you will. You need to learn some patience."

"I need you, baby. Please! I'm so wet for you."

A growl rumbled through my chest, escaping from my throat and she shivered. My fingers crawled lower, "Keep your tits down, your face in the lounger but lift your hips. I want to eat you just like this."

Her back rose and fell with excited breaths but without a word, she kept her face and tits on the lounger and arched her back, lifting her hips. Her pussy glistened alongside her oiled skin and I bit back the groan that threatened to erupt. I wanted to play. I wanted her to beg. If she knew how desperate I was to get inside her, it would be over before it started.

I hooked my arm under her stomach and shifted her higher, bringing her needy cunt level with my face, and buried my face between the cheeks of her ass. The smell of her arousal surrounded me and the taste of her juices hit my tongue. Sweet, tangy, sexy. It consumed me.

I licked her entrance, blew across her clit and dipped my tongue inside. Spreading her wider, I nuzzled her ass with my face as I moved my fingers around to circle her little bundle of nerves, bring her closer to the edge.

"You come with me inside you," I reminded her.

I needed to feel it. Needed to feel her walls tighten, and quiver around my cock.

I ached, I throbbed. The head of my dick was an angry shade of purple, pleading with me to let him inside. Minutes, hours, I ate at Carlie's pussy until her moans turns to pleasured cries and I knew she was struggling to hold back.

"You ready for me, pretty baby?"

She sobbed, "More than ready, Blake. God! Please! I need you to fuck me."

I plunged inside.

Heaven.

Fucking heaven, the way she instantly gripped the edges of the lounger, threw her head back and screamed my name into the seclusion. Her drenched cunt tightening, quivering and gushing around my cock. I pounded into her, gripping the cheeks of her ass hard enough to leave bruises and grunting out my approval.

"Up, Carlie," I growled. "You know how I want you."

Her orgasm was still sweeping through her, shivers wracked her body but she managed to shift herself to her knees. She lifted herself up, hooked her arm around my neck and turned just her face towards me, all the while still keeping my cock deep inside her pussy. I reached around to her front, pinching and rolling her nipples as I kept up my thrusts. She whimpered as I took her mouth in a bruising kiss. Dropping my hands from her tits to the apex of thighs, I spread her open with one hand and caressed her clit with the other, building her again.

"Let go, pretty baby," I whispered.

"Come with me, Blake."

She turned her face into my neck and bit down, hard. The shock of pain made me growl and slam my cock to the root inside her.

"Oh my god!" She cried, and I silently agreed.

My blood heated, from my toes to my chest to my balls and everywhere in between as my shaft lengthened insider her and my cum leaked from my body, coating her throbbing inner walls.

Panting, she breathed out, "I love you, my handsome husband."

"I love you too, my beautiful wife."

*I'm sorry, I don't understand you. My colleague speaks English and he will be back soon.

**Thank you, do you understand?

***My name is Carlie, and yours?

****Oh thank goodness. My name is Catrina. I beg you to tell me what you need. If you have a car reserved, I need your name, deposit and proof of identification.

***** I cannot wait to make love to my husband.

CHAPTER
Two

June 2012 - Three years before

After waiting for over a month. I could finally let her in on the surprise.

I had Carlie in the passenger seat next to me, driving towards the outskirts of town, so I could give her one of the things I knew she really wanted and I felt like an amazing husband.

She, on the other hand, was scowling at me.

I pursed my lips and kept my eyes on the road, not letting her see just how amused I was. She was annoyed because I wouldn't tell her where we were going or why we were going there. Not a fan of surprises, apparently.

I knew that, of course, we'd been together for nine years and married for seven. I was fairly certain I knew everything about her by that point. That though, was why I wasn't telling her where we were going. I knew what her reaction would be, I knew the sounds she'd make and I didn't want to ruin any of that by letting her know before she could actually get her hands on it.

So I let her stew on it, and I let her be annoyed because it wouldn't last.

"Nearly there," I muttered.

She sighed, "I don't even know why you would bring me out here. There's nothing here but factories and car dealerships..."

She drifted off, then I saw the light start to dawn.

Her shoulders straightened and her hands gripped the seat belt as the Mazda showroom came into view. Her eyes flicked to me, then back to the building. Hope flared.

"Blake?"

I ignored her, parked the car and got out.

"Blake?" She called again, jogging to keep up with me in my strides.

"*Blake?!*"

Inside, I walked straight to the main desk, asked for Pete and then turned to my wife.

"Just wait," I said. "Few more minutes, pretty baby. Then you can stop being pissed at me."

Her eyes narrowed but her body was telling the truth, she had an idea of what I'd done and she couldn't wait to see.

In less than five minutes, I got *exactly* what I wanted, and so did she.

"Oh my god!" She squealed and I laughed out loud at her shocked expression. "Blake, it's beautiful!"

"It's yours," I confirmed.

She threw her arms around my neck and squeezed, jumping up to wrap her legs around my waist. She kissed my neck and ran her fingers through the back of my hair.

"It's the best thing ever! I love it, and I love you."

I'd just given her the keys to her brand new Mazda MX-5 Miata, the car she had been throwing hints at me about for months. It was a pretty car, definitely made for a woman. I couldn't afford it outright but seeing as I was paying for the monthly payments and I'd paid the deposit, it was definitely a credit-worthy gift. For the smile she gave me, I'd have bought her two.

She was changing. Or maybe I was.

I couldn't put my finger on why but things were just...different.

Work took over my life and Carlie's obsession with being perfect was putting strain on our relationship that just wasn't there before. Call it cowardice, call it ridiculous, but I bought her the car to make her happy in the hopes that it would improve our relationship. The way she climbed me like a monkey told me I'd made the right choice.

She liked pretty things. I could give them to her. It should be as simple as that.

"I love you too, Carlie. Now here," I placed the keys in the palm. "Go take it for a drive, see how she moves."

She grinned and closed her hand into a fist, sliding her legs down from around my waist and stepping back. Walking around the vehicle, running her fingers along the gleaming silver paint, she looked transfixed.

"You like it?" I asked, even though I already knew the answer.

"Like it? Blake, you know how much I wanted this car. *Every* woman wants this car and I have it. The girls are going to be so jealous!"

I hid my wince. That wasn't exactly my aim when I ordered it. I wanted her to have the car *for her*. To make *her* happy. Not as a toy for her to show how perfect her life was, to make people jealous. I opened my mouth to tell her that, but she spoke first.

"You are so getting lucky for this later. I'm going to ride you so hard that you won't be able to walk tomorrow."

All thoughts of chastising her for wanting to make people jealous fled. I glanced over my shoulder to make sure Pete had gone back inside. He had.

The power of her hold over me was obvious and she knew how to work that.

"In that case, get your ass in that car, drive it into town and take a visit to *Ann Summers.* You can't just throw that out there when I'm about to go to work and expect me not to think about it for the next twelve hours. Stock up on toys, baby. Get some of that strawberry flavoured stuff too, I'm in the mood to play."

Her eyes glazed over and I knew she was remembering what happened last time. We both liked to play. Not whips, chains or clamps. Not my thing. But exploring, toys, and making her come so hard that it usually took hours afterwards for her to stop shaking. Yeah.

Fuck yeah.

I loved that.

Her mouth, her pussy, her ass. I owned them all. They belonged to me and she offered them freely.

Just not as often anymore and for some reason, that bothered her a lot more than it bothered me. I mean, we'd been married for seven years and I worked twelve hours a day, we didn't have the *time* to fuck like animals anymore. It sucked, but it was the reality.

Her words though, *'I'm going to ride you so hard that you can't walk tomorrow'*.

She'd do it too. She was a firecracker when she let loose. My shift at work was going to feel like the longest twelve hours of my life. That feeling only became more frustrating when she leaned forward, brushed her lips across mine in a whisper of a kiss, and whispered, "Quiero tu boca en mí, quiero tus dedos en mí y quiero ver tu cara como me llena. Me encanta como te siento dentro de mí. Sólo te quiero, mi esposo maravilloso."

I shivered. Seven years.

Seven years and the sound of her speaking in a beautiful foreign language still affected me the way it did before she learnt how to do it fluently.

"What does that mean?" I asked, not understanding a word, only knowing what the words were doing to my body.

"I want your mouth on me, I want your fingers in me, and I want to watch your face as you fill me. I only love you, my wonderful husband," She translated.

Maybe it wasn't the language she used, maybe it wasn't the way she said it, maybe it was just the words.

Those fucking words.

"Get in the car, Carlie," I sucked in a shaky breath, barely holding on to my last shred of control. "Get in the car, go to Ann Summers, enjoy the drive and do *not* look back this way until I've gone to work. If you don't leave now, we'll be leaving your present here and taking my car to the nearest secluded area so I can fuck you on the backseat."

She wrinkled her nose.

Cute. I liked that.

She'd rather fuck in the backseat than leave.

"Go, Carlie," I gave a light shove on the shoulder and turned her towards the car.

She got in and she drove away.

I breathed deeply, attempting to calm myself. My cock was hard, throbbing and if it didn't calm down, I wouldn't be able to walk, let alone work. It took a while, longer than it should have, but when my erotic thoughts temporarily faded...I went to work.

Concentrating was impossible.

I decided against doing school or home visits, mainly for the fact that there was no way I was in any sort of state to be around other people. My team, yeah, that was fine. But a room full of strangers? No.

I wanted to be at home. I wanted to be inside my wife.

Annoyingly, due to a last minute emergency call-out, I was still assisting the team at the end of my shift. Nine pm came and went, I grew increasingly frustrated and for the first time ever, I really, really despised my job. Being a firefighter meant any plans I'd made were often thwarted because, unsurprisingly, the job didn't come with a routine.

By eleven pm, I was exhausted, dirty and my eyes were fighting to stay open on the drive home. Frankly, all I wanted to do was strip down to my boxers, climb into bed and sleep for twenty four hours.

Pulling up outside our house, I noted all the lights were off.

Odd, I thought Carlie would be waiting up for me. Instead, I found her lying on top of the duvet on our bed, legs spread, naked other than a tiny white g-string. Strawberry flavoured lubricant lay on the bedside table, vibrator next to her hip.

She would have been the perfect vision of eroticism.

If she wasn't snoring quietly in her sleep.

I chuckled, typical.

I stripped down to my boxers, threw back the blankets and pulled Carlie into me as I covered the both us with the duvet. She snuggled into me, mumbling under her breath.

I sighed and closed my eyes, sleep sounded amazing.

CHAPTER
Three

June 2015 – Present day

"Congratulations, Blake!"

I grinned at Matt's outburst and swept the streams of paper off my shoulders from the party poppers they'd thrown at me, they must have known before I did.

I'd just been promoted to station manager and I couldn't have been more proud, or relieved. At thirty-five, I'd already been a firefighter for sixteen years and I was starting to feel it. I hated to admit it, but I just didn't have the energy, or stamina, to fight along with the younger lads anymore. I loved my job though, so being promoted, getting to still be a part of the team, albeit behind a desk, I was ecstatic.

"Thanks," I sighed.

Dave scoffed, "Don't act so relieved, we all knew that job was yours from the second Ian announced his retirement."

His words were true, there really wasn't anyone else suitable for the job but that didn't mean it was a guarantee. I just shrugged at him, ignored their playful jeers and pulled out my phone.

"Did you get it?" Carlie answered.

My wife. My love. My heart. We'd been married ten years and I still had to smile every time I heard her voice.

"Just call me 'boss man', baby," I joked.

I moved my phone away from my ear and her high-pitched squeal came through the line, "Congratulations! I knew you'd get it! I'm so happy for you."

"Thank you. I'll probably be home late because I'm going to start getting my head around all the new duties, but I'll see you later ok?"

She was silent for a few beats, then she sighed deeply, "Yeah ok, I'll put dinner in the microwave so you can just reheat it when you get home."

"Love you," I called before she hung-up. She returned the sentiment and ended the call.

Twenty minutes later, I sat behind my new desk and stared out the window. I'd hadn't been able to go on call-outs with the rest of the guys for over a month anyway because of a lingering shoulder injury, but watching them all suit up as the alarms rang around the station...

It hurt.

I already missed the action, the adrenaline.

"Doesn't feel good, does it?" Ian's voice sounded from the doorway.

I shook my head, no, it really didn't feel good.

"It'll pass. You know as well as I do that there'll be times they still need you out in the field. The first time they do, it'll hit you like a ton of bricks. You have to be able to stand by their side and know that you can fight just as hard as the next man. You're still young enough to do that, but old enough to be better at your job from right here. That shoulder injury should have healed by now. It would've been too, if you were ten years younger and that's the point. Try not to linger on those thoughts of being left behind, because those guys still need you, just not in the same way anymore."

"Did it feel the same for you?" I asked, curious if it was just me.

"Yes, and no. I was well into my forties before I took the station manager role. I knew it was my time to call it a day. Frankly, I hung-on longer than I should have. There were a couple of times right at the end of my days in the field, when the team was dragging me along with them. I'm lucky I didn't cause any incidents," this surprised me. Ian was always the guy who played by the rules and didn't take any chances. "No one wants to admit when their time is up, Blake. It's painful and some people just can't take the feeling of not being needed in the same way anymore. You're doing the right thing though and you're still a huge role-model for the rest of the team. Every single one of those guys out there looks up to you, even the older ones. Don't let them down by sulking about what you can't do anymore."

I nodded, "I won't let them down. It'll just take some time to get used to it, I guess."

He opened his mouth to speak, but was interrupted by loud whistling from the six guys still left in the station. I stood from my chair and strode around my desk.

"What the...?"

Ian's smiling eyes came to mine, "Fuck you for moaning about stupid shit! You really are a lucky son of a bitch, Blake."

He shook his head and opened the door wider, stepping outside. My eyes swept the station, following the guys' line of vision, I had to do a double-take when I spotted Carlie making her way towards me. My eyes dropped to her lips where she was smiling, her shoulders, her slender waist and finally, her long, tanned, toned legs. Damn right, I was a lucky son of a bitch, but I didn't understand what she was doing there.

She was stunning. She always had been. She wore her long blonde hair in a twist at the base of her neck and she was wearing heavy make-up, the kind she wore for a night out.

Her feet were dressed in the highest pair of strappy heels I'd ever seen her wear and I swear I could see a glimpse of lace under the edge of her thigh-length coat. Eating up the distance between us in seconds, she slid her hands up my chest and linked them behind my neck. In heels, she was almost at eye-level with me, so she wasted no time in pulling me to her for a kiss.

In shock, I didn't open my mouth. I felt her tongue touch my lips but she froze when she realised I wasn't moving. Ignoring the catcalls from the guys, I put my hand to the small of her back, pushed her inside the office and lowered the blinds.

"That was quite the show out there! What are you doing here?" I asked.

Her face fell and I instantly felt guilty, "I'm sorry. I'm happy to see you, obviously. But I thought you were working today."

"I was, but I finished early because I knew you were waiting to hear about this job and I wanted to come here and surprise you no matter the outcome. Celebrations or commiserations, your wife should be there, Blake! I know it was a tough decision for you to apply for this job but I'm so proud of you. I didn't want to wait for hours for you to get home, so I thought I'd come give you my congratulations in person," her fingers ran lightly along my arms as she spoke, almost soothing. "Are you saying that I should not have bothered?"

One of her perfectly-shaped eyebrows raised and I found myself stuck. Truth was, her being there was a distraction that I didn't have time for, as bad as that sounds. I knew she'd clearly made an effort though, so I cleared my throat and smiled. I hoped she couldn't tell that it wasn't entirely real.

"It's a great surprise, babe. You look amazing too," she did. She looked incredible and if we'd have been anywhere but my place of work, I'd have been looking for the closest private place to get her naked.

Her grin lit up her face.

"Usted no ha visto la mejor broca todavía..." she muttered as she slid the belt on her coat open and slowly started undoing the buttons. *You haven't seen the best bit yet.*

I swallowed. As each button popped open, revealing what was underneath. Or more importantly, what *wasn't* underneath. My cock stirred behind my slacks and my eyebrows shot up. She stood before me in a see-through, lacy, white corset, sheer white g-string and matching suspender belt. The coat landed in a heap at her feet but I couldn't tear my eyes away from her hips. The way the whole ensemble showcased her amazing figure, I could hardly breathe.

"You look..." I broke off, not able to finish my sentence.

Her eyes flashed with wickedness and she swayed her hips slightly, running her fingers along the top of the corset, "You like?"

"I..."

Alarms blared throughout the station and I heard Ian barking orders at the firefighters. I shook my head.

"Jesus Christ," I muttered, what the fuck was she thinking? "*Jesus Christ!* Get your coat on, Carlie. You need to go, I have a job to do."

She flinched at my tone, but bent to retrieve her coat. I bit back my groan as she flashed me her smooth, rounded ass.

"Why? It's not like you have to go out with them," she sulked.

I snapped. It was uncalled for and out of line, but it annoyed me that she didn't understand and she clearly hadn't thought it through at all.

"You look hot, babe. Gorgeous. But I'm at work for fuck sake! What did you think was going to happen?" She opened her mouth but I talked over her. "What? You'd come in here looking like every guys fucking wet dream and I'd fuck you over my new office desk? Fucking hell, Carlie! Thanks, but you've gotta go. I don't have time for this."

Hurt filled her eyes and I winced. I'd never been great at thinking before I spoke.

"Fuck you, Blake. I was *trying* to do something nice, something *fun* for a change," she explained.

The door handle rattled and her face lost all colour as she scrambled to do her coat up.

Ian popped his head around the door, I couldn't miss the flash of shock in his eyes as he noticed Carlie doing up the last of her buttons, "Team's already moving out. Head-on smash on Windward Place, one of the cars is on fire and there's a man trapped in the front seat of the other car."

I nodded but barely glanced in his direction.

"I'm just going to go," Carlie murmured. "I'll see you later at home."

Scrubbing my hands down my face, I let out

breathe of air, "Babe," I grabbed her hand before she could leave. "I'll try not to be too late home, ok? I'm sorry this didn't work out. I love you though."

She closed her eyes and shook her head, looking somewhere between upset and disappointed. I hated that look on her face, knowing I'd put it there, made me feel worse.

She left without another word and I felt like the worst husband in the world. I made a mental note to grab a bunch of flowers at some point.

The house was silent when I arrived home at eight, causing me to frown. I was only an hour late, Carlie wasn't usually in bed that early.

I changed into a t-shirt and loose pair of joggers, turned the microwave on to heat my dinner and leant back against the kitchen counter. The rest of my day at work had flown by but that annoying voice in my head kept whispering that I was doing the wrong thing; that I should have been at home with my wife. When you've spent your whole life trying to be the best you can in your career, it's easy to forget what's really important. Part of me knew I was failing at being a good husband, the rest of me thought that Carlie should be more understanding.

Life was about compromise. Yet, we were both terrible at it. I wanted to be perfect in my career, she wanted to portray the perfect marriage. I truly didn't know if we could a find a way to have both. Realistically, I knew there was no such thing as 'perfection'. But doesn't everyone have dreams? Aspirations?

I shouldn't have to give up on mine because my wife was easily bored.

I wolfed down my dinner, barely tasting a thing due to my disconcerting thoughts. With my eye-lids feeling heavy, I made my way to the bedroom, sliding into bed in silence. Carlie lay next to me, head propped up on the pillows, book in her hands. Call me a coward, but I just didn't know what to say to her.

I heard her loud sigh and tensed, "This isn't working anymore, is it?"

"What's not working anymore?" I asked, my pulse raging in my ears as I waited for her to explain.

"This! Us," she cried. "We're just *existing* together. We don't date anymore, we hardly talk anymore and for god sake we haven't had sex in over two months! I get it, we've been together more than twelve years so we're not going to be screwing like bunnies anymore but damn it, Blake! You made me look a complete fool today. I'm still a woman and I think you're forgetting that."

"That's ridiculous," I scoffed. She was obviously just overthinking things, I loved her just as much as the day we got married and I told her that every day. She turned to me, her eyes were wet with unshed tears but her face was set with determination.

"Is it, Blake? Is it ridiculous? I can already see that you don't understand. Let me guess, you tell me you love me every day, so I'm just overthinking things. Am I right?"

It should be surprising that she knew exactly what I was thinking, but it wasn't. From day one, she'd always been great at reading my face. She usually knew what I was going to say before I said it.

Shrugging, I replied, "I may be thinking that, but I also know I'm right, Carlie. There's nothing wrong with our marriage really. Sure, things have changed but that's life, darling. We grow and we adapt. Why don't you have a look online, see if there's any new classes going on down at the community centre, you could start a new hobby or something?"

I thought it was a good suggestion. I was apparently wrong. She scrambled from the bed, giving me a sexy little flash of her ass for the second time that day - definitely not for my benefit though. Swinging around, her eyes shot flames in my direction.

"*You think I need to get a hobby because my husband won't fuck me?*" She screeched and the sound travelled straight through me. "You're...ugh, you're a prick, Blake. *Listen to me*, I'm telling you something is missing these days. Answer me one question, when was the last time I laughed?"

Her random question had me stumped. How was supposed to answer that? My blank look must have told her everything she needed to know.

"Don't you see? This isn't a marriage anymore, Blake. I love you, I always have but this isn't healthy. Are you just not attracted to me anymore? Is that it?"

I fought the eye-roll that threatened to escape. Women. Completely and utterly crazy.

"Don't ask stupid questions, Carlie. That won't get us anywhere."

"Get anywhere. *Get anywhere?* You're forgetting that this is YOU, Blake. Unless it's your idea, your choice or your decision, we *never* get anywhere. I don't make idol threats, you know this, but I can't live like this anymore."

My eyebrows shot to my hairline and my heart stopped beating, "So what exactly are you saying, Carlie. This day, the day that I hit the height of my career, the thing I've worked for all my life, you're telling me...what? That you want to leave me? Divorce me?"

Her shoulders slumped like they were carrying the weight of the world.

"Not exactly. You think I want to leave you? That I'd rather be a thirty-three year old divorcee? Of course not. I'm just saying that things need to change, Blake. They *have* to."

"So let's go on a date or something. It's really not as terrible as you seem to think, babe. Just tell me what you want and I'll give it to you."

Her eyes remained sad, but her lips tipped up at the corners, "I shouldn't have to tell you, and I guess that's the point. But if you're willing to try, then so am I," she hit the bed and snuggled back under the covers, sliding her arm across my stomach in the same movement. "I love you, Blake. No matter what, for better or worse, right? We'll get through this."

With my heart feeling heavy and confusion swirling in my brain, I kissed her forehead and repeated her words back to her.

"I love you too, pretty baby. For better or worse."

CHAPTER
Four

"Harder, Blake."

I sped up my thrusts, feeling beads of sweat run down my back. I gripped her thighs in my palms and held them against my chest, ploughing into her slick pussy over and over.

"Please honey, *give it to me harder*," she whimpered.

"Fuck," I pushed deeper. "Any fucking harder and I'll break you!"

Curling her feet around my neck, she growled, "Fuck me, Blake. Hard, fast, brutal. Fuck me, break me and make me *yours*. I need to feel like you to own me again."

At the reminder of the night before, because I knew she was doubting us, I became desperate. I pinched each nipple between thumb and forefinger, twisted and pulled. Her back arched, her pussy clamped down around my cock and a long moan escaped her parted lips.

Sorry neighbours, but a man has a job to do.

Moving one hand to her throat, I squeezed lightly as I kept pounding into her, "You *are* mine. You've been mine since the day you said 'I do,' and you'll be mine for *fucking* ever."

My balls tightened, my rhythm faltered, but I

breathed out, "I will never let you leave me."

Eyes glazed over, hair sticking to her damp forehead and skin flushed pink, Carlie had never looked so fucking gorgeous. She bit down on her bottom lip, closed her eyes and clenched thighs as her orgasm washed over her. I thrust deep and let go of her legs, lowering myself over her. My cock throbbed and I emptied myself inside her.

"That was…"

"I know," I agreed. There were no words.

"Te echaba de menos, Blake. *I missed you.* I know this doesn't fix us, but at least we know that we're still here somewhere."

With nothing else to say, I just smiled down at her, then sat back on my calves. Glancing at the clock, I was going to be pushing it to get to work on time. I patted Carlie on the hip and told her I loved her, then shrugged into my shirt and slacks. About to do my tie in the mirror, I noticed Carlie still hadn't moved.

"You just going to lie there all day?" I joked, knowing she was probably going to head to the gym before work.

She sighed, looking wistful, "No, just thinking."

"Oh dear," I laughed.

She wrinkled her nose at me, but dragged herself up from the bed, groaning with the movement.

"Maybe there is nothing wrong with us, maybe we are just getting too old to be doing it like that now!"

"Speak for yourself! I'm about to go and do a twelve hour shift, I've got this. I'm not old."

She grinned, looking so much like the Carlie I married, "That's what you think!"

I whipped her lightly with my tie and scowled before turning back to the mirror. We finished getting ready in comfortable silence. I left the house with a smile on my face and feeling better than I had in months. If an early morning fuck and five minutes of conversation was all she needed to be happy, I could give that to Carlie. With pleasure.

So why did I still have that feeling of unsettlement in the pit of my stomach?

I chose to ignore it.

My phone bleeped with a text alert within an hour of being at work. Not that this was unusual of course, it wasn't. Carlie's name flashed on the screen.

Carlie: *Do you think it's weird that we don't have children?*

My eyebrows rose. Was it weird that we didn't have children? No, not really. Was it weird that in twelve years of being together, ten of those married, we'd never spoken about it for any length of time? Definitely. The fact that she'd thrown it out there in a text message, put me on edge. I figured the conversation deserved a phone call. She answered on the third ring.

"Hi, honey."

"Why would you text me that?"

She gave me a nervous giggle, "I don't know. It's weird don't you think? Maybe that's what we're missing. We're in our thirties now and we don't have to do the school run, go to PTA meetings. We don't have any drawings on the fridge or badly painted Christmas tree decorations. I just started thinking about it, maybe we should start trying for a baby."

My blood pressure started to rise, I was more than aware that I had to be really careful with how I responded.

"Carlie, this isn't the right time to talk about this darling. We will soon though, ok?"

"Oh," she paused. "Oh right, of course. You're at work, silly me! We'll talk about it when you get home later."

"No...I," I jumped in before she could hang up. "Honey, I don't mean later. I mean, you're right, we need to make things right with *us* first, before we talk about babies or whatever, ok?"

The silence from the other end of the line stretched on. I prompted her to speak.

"Sure. Right, yeah, sure, ok. Talk to you later."

She hung up.

I fought the urge to bang my head against the desk. One step forward, two steps back. It felt like someone had flicked a switch in her brain and now everything had to be done at either warp speed, or not at all. I started to realise that it wasn't just about me failing her as a husband anymore. It still played a part; a huge part, I suspected, but it wasn't just that. With a sigh, I made the decision to put it all to the back of my mind and concentrate on work.

With four home visits and two school talks, the day dragged on and on until, for once, I couldn't wait to get home. Technically speaking, I didn't have to attend the visits, but the thought of sitting in an office all day just made me tense. It wasn't going to happen. Instead, I watched the guys talk through home safety with two elderly couples and two young families, then tortured myself at the schools. Who knew teenage kids were such vile creatures?

So to say I wasn't in the best of moods when I arrived home is a slight understatement. Never a good thing when tensions are already high.

Thankfully, though I knew I shouldn't feel that way, Carlie wasn't home yet. I just needed the quiet, the solidarity, to think about everything that was happening and why.

I stood under the shower, my head leaning against the tiles wondering how I'd gone from being the luckiest guy in the world to feeling like I had the weight of the Earth on my shoulders. Had I missed the signs? Was it really as sudden as it seemed? Too many questions. I didn't have the answers and really, I couldn't be sure that Carlie did either. She seemed so up and down. Happy, then upset. Calm, then angry. It was messing with my mind.

Hearing the front door close, I knew it was time to face this head on. No more craziness. I quickly towel dried and stepped out of the bathroom, tying the towel around my waist. Carlie stood on the landing and attempted to push past me. Blocking her with my arm, I kissed her cheek.

"Hello my darling wife, how was your day?"

"Fuck off, Blake," she snapped, then slammed the bathroom door.

That went well.

I scrubbed my hands down my face, moved to our bedroom and threw on some joggers. Life wasn't supposed to be this difficult. Feet stomping down the hall alerted me to her presence and I sucked in a slow breath. Time to try again.

"Honey..."

"I don't want to talk about it, Blake. So you don't want kids, fine, whatever, you still should have told me that sooner. There's no point discussing it now."

She slammed the wardrobe doors and whirled away from me, "We'll just...carry on as we are."

"I never once said I didn't want kids, Carlie.

You're overreacting again. Do you really think this, this *thing* between us is going to get any better, by bringing a child into the world? I'm just saying we need time, honey. I'm not saying never."

"How much time, Blake? A year, two...five? Time isn't on our side with this. My biological clock is ticking!"

I paused, getting nowhere with the conversation. The something occurred to me.

"Why do you want this so much, so quickly? You've hardly mentioned kids in the last ten years and now we need to get started straight away, why?"

"I'm getting old!" She cried, throwing her hands up. "Women are supposed to have babies and families and, and, I don't know!"

I knew my smile was sad when I replied, "Exactly, Carlie. You don't know. We can't make life changing decisions on a whim. Whatever this is, whatever is making you so unhappy, we'll fix it first. I promise you. When you figure out what it is that you need, I'll do it for you. Wherever you want to go, whoever you want to see, fuck! Absolutely anything, Carlie. I'll get it, do it, find it and fix it. I just want my wife back, ok?"

Her lower lip trembled and her eyes filled. I never could deal well with a woman crying, "Don't do that! Don't cry!"

"I'm sorry! I'm so sorry. I just don't know what's wrong with me! My head is all over the place, Blake. You're right, I know you're right but it's not as simple as just asking for something. Especially when I don't know what that something is."

I pulled her into my arms. Honestly, I was starting to agree with the majority of the male sex. Women truly are crazy.

"How about, and hear me out...you just stop worrying about it? Whatever it is, will work itself out, yeah? Just remember, I love you, and we'll make this work."

She sighed, "I love you too, babe. And I'm sorry."

Crisis averted. For now.

CHAPTER
Five

"Blake..."

"I'm right here, Carlie."

It was a week after the last drama and things had been blessedly content, almost suspiciously so. Carlie was smiling, whistling around the house and touching me at every opportunity. She just seemed almost *too* happy. It was better than complaining about every breath I took though, so I just left it alone.

"I've been thinking about something, and you can say no," I cut her off with a laugh.

And here it comes.

"You really shouldn't tell me I can say no before you've even said what you want."

I thought she would laugh, she didn't. Her face was a mask of nerves, with a weird undercurrent of excitement. Call me curious, I needed to know what that was all about.

"Shoot, what's up?"

"I had this idea, and call me crazy," *never a good sign.* "But I really think maybe it could be fun, and it's something I want to try."

"Ok..." I said slowly, hinting at her to go on.

"What do you think about, I mean, how would you feel, if we, maybe,"

"Jesus, Carlie! Spit it out!"

"I want to have a threesome."

Whoa. Well I wasn't expecting that. Flashes of pornographic images crossed my vision and my cock twitched. Silently reminding myself that I wasn't supposed to be a horny teenage boy anymore, I frowned at her.

"It's an... interesting idea, babe. But, and please don't take this the wrong way, you can get a little jealous sometimes. Just last week when we were shopping and that woman asked me to grab her something from the top shelf, you were in a bad mood for hours afterwards and I hardly even spoke to her!"

"That's not true! I was in a bad mood because I was standing *right there* and she stared at your ass the whole time!"

I tilted my head and gave her a look, "Even so, she was just looking. I didn't do anything wrong and you gave me the silent treatment for a good few hours."

"I was just mad. I wasn't mad *at you*, just mad in general!" She explained, as if that made it any better.

"Exactly! Say we do this, how are you going to feel if I touch another woman, if she touches me? I really don't think it's a good idea."

Really, my brain was screaming at me that I was passing up on a huge opportunity, but there was this niggling thought in my mind that actually, I didn't even *want* to touch another woman. I was married for god sake! Look, but don't touch. That was a rule that I'd learned to live by.

"No, that wasn't what I..."

I interrupted, "Babe, seriously, it's really not a good idea."

"Blake! Will you listen? I didn't mean with another woman, I meant with another man."

Wait, what?

My jaw dropped. She couldn't be serious. No way, no how, was I letting another man in our bed.

"Are you crazy? You must be, certifiably crazy. There's no way I'm doing *that!*"

Her hands came up in a placating gesture, "I know, I know. It does sound crazy, but think about it. I'm not asking you to touch him or anything. I'm just...well, I just thought that it would be fun."

"You're basically stood there telling me that I should be ok with my wife wanting to fuck another guy! How could you ever think that I would be ok with this?"

"That's not..."

"No, no, *no*. It's not going to happen. I can't...I just don't even believe you'd ask for that! I'm going to work, I'll see you later."

"Blake..."

I left the house shaking my head. The hit to my ego was only slightly less painful than the thought of Carlie with another man. Days before, she's asking me if I don't find her attractive anymore, then she's basically telling me I'm not enough for her. Talk about a mind-fuck.

I still hadn't shook the negative thoughts by the time I got to the station, the guys picked up on it instantly.

"Hey, Bossman! Who pissed in your Cornflakes?"

"Fuck off, Marc. Haven't you got a pole that needs shining?"

Grabbing his crotch, he leered at me jokingly,

"Damn right. Damn, fucking, right!"

I cracked a smile and rolled my eyes as I shook my head. No matter how old we are, men will always turn into fifteen year old boys when there is the potential for a dick joke. Don't let anyone tell you any differently.

"Get your hand off your dick and get to work!"

He mock saluted, "Yes, sir!"

Slouching down into my office chair, I frowned when I realised that, again, within five minutes of being at the station, I was happy. It was my comfort zone, the place I was in charge and I loved the guys. Maybe Carlie had a point, my attachment to work just wasn't healthy for our marriage, but it worked for me. Did I really have to sacrifice one for the other?

I couldn't change who I was, that much I was sure of. I wasn't all that big on compromising with it either. My job paid the bills, paid for our holidays and the majority of our lives. Carlie worked, but she kept that pay check for herself. Her gym membership, hair, nails, and new clothes every week, she had to pay for them somehow. I didn't resent it, or I hadn't, until then. Couldn't she see how unreasonable it was to complain about the one thing that kept her living the good life that she had become accustomed to?

She was a daddy's girl. Her dad, Roy, would hit the roof if he thought I was not 'providing' for his little girl. Frankly, I wouldn't have it any other way. I liked being the main earner. Call me sexist, but a man should look after his woman. Don't get me wrong, I'm not stuck back in the 1940's or anything, I didn't care that she worked and I didn't expect dinner on the table the minute I got home. She did her own thing and I loved that.

I just liked being the man of the house.

So her asking me to allow another man into our lives, into our bed, no. I just couldn't do it.

Work flew by without major incident. Admittedly, I hung around longer than I needed to at the end of my shift because I just couldn't face what was waiting for me at home. I was dreading any form of conversation. Unfortunately, I had to leave at some point though.

Soft music played from the direction of the kitchen when I entered the house and I followed the sound, hoping and praying Carlie had forgotten all about her ridiculous ideas. The table was set, candles were lit and Carlie sat at the end of the table with a shy smile touching her lips.

"I made dinner," she explained, needlessly.

"I can see that," I said slowly, wondering if this was her way of softening me up to her plans. I threw my bag down on the counter and sat opposite her at the table.

"I'm sorry about this morning, I don't want to argue with you anymore, Blake."

I shook my head, "I'm not arguing. You should have known before the idea even entered your head that I would say no."

"I just think it could be fun, Blake! Something new and exciting. This could really help *us* come closer together."

My fork hit the plate with a clatter and Carlie jumped. The gorgeous chicken casserole suddenly tasting like sour milk in my mouth.

"It *could* be fun. It *could* be new and exciting. It *could* help us be closer together. Funny Carlie, that sounds suspiciously like you're still thinking about doing it."

She swallowed, "I am, Blake. I was speaking to

the owner of the gym and he was saying..."

"Stop," I interrupted, shoving my chair back and standing. "Not only did I say no, I clearly told you that even the idea makes me feel sick and I have absolutely no intention of doing anything of the kind and you have *still* been making plans with some vain asshole from the gym? Are you out of your fucking mind? What the fuck?"

"It isn't like that! I was just talking! He was just saying..." I broke in again.

"Oh I bet I know exactly what he was saying, bet I know what he was thinking too. Bored wife looking for a little side action. You're beautiful, Carlie. You know that and *he* knows that. He was probably thinking he'll convince you to try for a threesome and knowing that any straight man in his right mind would say no, the seed is already planted for you. Won't take much effort to convince you that a quick fuck on the side wouldn't hurt. Who's ever going to know?"

"You're wrong! He's not that guy! He's a friend and he was just trying to help. Trust me, he doesn't need to play games to sleep with people, Blake. He's had sex with half the members at the gym!"

My eyes bulged. Could she really not see that she'd just explained exactly the point I was making. She dropped her head to stare at the table.

"I know how it sounds but he's just, I don't know, open about that stuff. But he's a good person, Blake. He's been like therapy or something, for me. He doesn't make moves, he doesn't touch me and he doesn't even flirt! He wants to help!"

"Wait, wait, wait, have you *asked* him to do this?"

She bit her lip, it should have been sexy, but my blood was way past boiling and I had no reaction.

"Sort of," I opened my mouth to cut in, but she kept talking. "No, wait, let me explain. I just said I liked the idea and he said to give him a call if we wanted to do it. That's all."

"That's all? *That's all?!* Fucking hell, Carlie! You are completely unbelievable. How can you not see how selfish you've been? How do you think it affects *me* to know that you've been telling some other guy about our sex life - or lack of? This guy must think he's onto a right winner with you."

She stood too and crossed the room to stand in front of me, "For the last time. He's not like that. I just needed someone to talk to, Blake! And he was there for me! You're making out like I'm cheating on you!"

"On me? No. But you've definitely cheated on our relationship, on our trust. Just because you say you haven't done anything wrong, yet, doesn't mean that's true. You betrayed my trust and you've allowed this guy to lay all his groundwork. Don't deny it because it's fucking true."

Instead of replying, she stepped closer, her tits touched my chest and I inhaled.

"What are you doing?" I breathed out.

"I would never betray you, Blake. You're my husband and I love you," her hand snaked out to cup my cock behind my trousers. "He doesn't have me, you do. I own this cock, and you own my pussy. That's the way it is and the way it'll always be."

Fuck, she was playing me and I was going to fall for it.

"This isn't about having sex with someone else, clear that from your mind," considering I was pretty much incapable of thinking about anything other than the way her hand was curling around my cock, I could do that. "This is about *us*. About us trying something new, sharing a new experience, learning more about each other, exploring our sexual boundaries. I want to do this, Blake. Let's do it, just try, I think it might open your eyes. If I didn't think you'd love this, that this would be something incredible for *both* of us, then I wouldn't have even thought about it. I certainly wouldn't have suggested it to him *or* you."

Without giving me chance to respond, not that I could have, she pushed up onto her toes and kissed me. I didn't need any persuasion, my tongue swept in and her sweet mouth consumed me. We fought for control, the twist of her tongue matching mine, the grind of her hips driving me insane. She grabbed one of my hands and smoothed it along her thigh, delving under her skirt and I growled when I found her already wet.

"Imagine it, Blake," she whispered. "Imagine this, right now, but he's here, he's watching. He wants what's yours. You get to tease him and drive him insane with jealousy because he knows he'll never have it. He'll beg, he'll tell you how hot this is and how much he wishes he could touch us. What better way to tease, Blake? You'll tell him he can come closer, that he can have a single taste but he needs to remember that I don't belong to him. Because I'm yours, right? Only yours. Maybe you'll let him touch me here," her hand pushed my fingers deeper. "Or maybe only you can do that but he wants the taste, Blake. You'll push your fingers into his mouth and let him suck them clean. It's so hot, I'll be on fire and it'll be too much. I'll drop to my knees and suck your cock while he licks my taste off your fingers. Imagine it, Blake. Can you see it? That's just the start."

"Ok," I croaked, barely able to keep my feet. "Ok, ok, yeah, we'll do it."

She hopped up onto the kitchen counter, shoved my trousers down to my ankles and guided my straining cock to her entrance.

"Fuck me, Blake."

Hook, line and sinker.

She couldn't have played that any better.

God damn it.

CHAPTER
Six

I paced the lounge, wondering if maybe it was *me* who had lost their mind.

Instead of doing what I should have done and telling Carlie that sexual coercion is null and void when it involves something as monumental as a threesome with another man, I let her make her plans. Which, may I add, she didn't waste any time doing. It was the Saturday after I had agreed to her ridiculous idea and Carlie had me waiting around while she 'got herself ready'.

Is she fucking kidding me with this shit?

Honestly, I couldn't have felt like less of man. Waiting for *my wife* to get ready, to make herself look even more beautiful for another fucking guy. I was working myself up, and not in the way she wanted me to. I wasn't excited, or nervous at all. I was purely just pissed off. Seeing as the asshole who had agreed to come and be a part of...whatever it was, would be arriving any minute, I didn't have time to talk myself down.

The doorbell rang and Carlie shouted down for me to answer it. I was pretty certain that it wasn't possible to feel any more awkward, until she said that. Me answer the door to this guy? *Not* a good idea. I did it anyway.

I opened the door, stepped forward, and punched the stranger across the jaw. My fist connecting with his chin, it didn't feel nearly as good as it should have. He barely moved an inch. I shook out the pain in my hand and watched in confusion as the guy smiled, split lip and all.

"Not exactly the welcome I was expecting, but let's get all of your anger out now shall we?" His fingers came to his mouth and he winced when they came away bloody, "Nice shot though. I'm Zach."

He held out his hand. Like I was going to shake it? Fuck no.

My shoulders twitched with the need to punch him again, to try and rid him of the smugness that radiated from him. He was saved when Carlie came bounding down the stairs.

"Blake! What are you doing?" She sucked in a breath at, what I'm assuming was, *Zach's* split lip.

"Don't worry about it, beautiful. I could do with something to stop the bleeding though!"

The fucker smiled again and stepped around me to hug Carlie. Instantly, I knew that it was going to destroy me to go through with it. The guy was everything I wasn't. Never having worried about feeling self-conscious before, even in the slightest, I fought back the doubts in my mind.

He was broad shouldered, taller than me, but not by much and his face just *screamed* 'there isn't a person alive who doesn't want a piece of me'. He was what women's dreams were made of. No wonder Carlie wanted to play with him.

I hated him touching her and I just hated him. Carlie scowled at me over his shoulder. How was I the bad guy in the situation? He turns up to *my* house, in his gym gear, knowing his plan was to fuck my wife, and I'm in the wrong? No.

"Come through to the kitchen, we'll get that sorted. I'm sorry about him, he's having a few issues with this," she dismissed me.

"Don't," I said quietly. "Don't you dare, Carlie. I agreed to go along with this fucked up mess *for you.* I'm letting this fucker in our house *for you.* Right now, I'm holding onto my last shred of control and not letting my anger go, *for you.* So don't put that shit on me. Don't throw around words like 'issues' when this isn't about me. This is *all* about you. My thoughts on the matter are clear, now let's get this shit over with."

She didn't respond but she did have the sense to look guilty. So she should. Without sounding like the pussy she was making me out to be, it was tearing me apart inside.

"Does this bother you?" Considering I wasn't looking at him, Zach's question made my eyes fly to his. His hand snaked around the curve of Carlie's waist and he pulled her back into him. "Or what about this?"

That same hand climbed upwards; I ignored the fact that she had dressed up in some, sheer, lacy, red little corset thing and concentrated on her reaction. Her eyes had turned glassy, and her breathing was accelerating. Her face screamed nervous anticipation but her body was already paying attention. If I didn't look at his hands, if I didn't listen to the words that came out of his mouth, just reading her body's reactions was almost beautiful.

Realising that this guy was playing me, with my own wife's arousal, I reacted. I moved across the room, swung Carlie around into my arms and stepped back, putting a few feet of space between them. She yelped, but turned to face him, picking up on my signals.

"This isn't your game," I told Zach. "If we're doing this, we do it my way."

Panting for breath, Carlie wheezed out a suggestion that we should be talking first, setting some rules. I didn't want to talk to the guy. If he overstepped a boundary, if he pushed me too far, he'd just have to learn the rules along the way. Stupid maybe, but sitting down and having a discussion would just ruin me. I could let this play out, and I would.

Conjuring up the visions of Carlie's speech about this night, I carved out a plan in my head.

I gripped Carlie's hips and squeezed but kept my eyes on Zach, "She's beautiful, isn't she? How many times have you watched her work-out and thought 'I wish I could have her'? How many times have you gone home and jerked off to the thought of being able to do this?" I slipped my fingers along the edge of her panties and teased her entrance. "How many times have you thought about how it would feel to hear her moan your name as she comes? Or to watch her ride your cock like a pro?"

Other than a barely-noticeable lip twitch, he showed no outward reaction but I knew my words were affecting him. The way Carlie's inner walls were clenching around my fingers made me continue.

"Don't forget that I hold all the cards here. Your mind games won't work on me," I kept up my relentless assault on Carlie's senses as I spoke. "If you want to come closer, you ask *me*. You want to touch her, you ask *me*. You even want to *look* at her, you...ask...me. Or you can leave and just keep dreaming about it because you'll *never* get the reality. Understood?"

Carlie whimpered when I sped up my fingers, her juices coated my hand and Zach's eyes fell to her pussy. He nodded slowly, but his confidence didn't falter when he confirmed, "Understood."

I thought he'd immediately come closer, or ask to at least, but he didn't. Leaning against the opposite wall, he crossed his arms over his broad chest and stared. His eyes were hungry and his fists clenched, he was keeping his reaction in check. Carlie was right, I wanted to toy with him.

I sucked on the sensitive skin at the base of her neck and she moaned when I lightly twisted one nipple. Her hips moved in tandem with my fingers, she was searching for it. I wanted to toy with Zach, I wanted to toy with Carlie. The rush of control, of possession, was too strong.

"Look, Carlie. Look at him. You were right. My beautiful wife has him in the palm of her hand because he craves her. Open your legs wider, baby. Show him how wet you are, let him see how much it turns you on when I fuck you with my fingers. You want his mouth on your clit, you want him to suck you while I fuck you? You, baby, you need to make him beg for it."

"Blake..." She rasped, her body pleading with me. I wanted the words. I needed them.

"You know what I need, Carlie," I slowed my fingers and she mewled in protest.

Panting, she opened her eyes and stared at Zach.

"Zach," she began, "Please..."

His mouth pursed and he rested one foot back against the wall, "Please what, Carlie?"

Oh he was good, I'd give him that.

"I need, I need, Zach please!"

Biting down on his bottom lip, hiding a grin, he inched forward but stopped.

"What is it, Carlie? What do you want from me?"

"Beg him!" She cried. "Please, Zach! Please, I can't cope with it. Please, please..." She trailed off on a moan when I thrust my fingers inside hard and fast.

I held Zach's eyes, silently daring him. Could he do it? Could he sacrifice a little of his ego and beg me? Clenching his jaw, he edged forward again, stopping just short of touching Carlie and he fell to his knees.

"Please, Blake. Let me give her what she needs," he asked.

I raised one eyebrow, "What *she* needs?"

"What I need. What we *all* want...I'm begging you."

"You want it, pretty baby? You need it?" I whispered in Carlie's ear.

"Yes, yes! I need it, Blake!"

I parted her lips, showing Zach every inch of her glistening pussy, giving him one last tease before I let him have what he wanted.

"Do it. Lick her, Zach. And don't be gentle, fuck her with your mouth. Go on, do it."

With one last glance at my face, he moved forward and put his mouth on Carlie. She cried out and trembled in my arms, her legs giving way with the first lash of his tongue. My cock jumped painfully but I needed the ache to keep me grounded, to keep me from throwing Carlie down and fucking her like a rampant animal on the floor. If I did that, it would be over before it really got started.

Her hands fell to Zach's hair and she tugged him closer, grinding her hips into his face. Shocking me to the core, I realised that it wasn't just her reactions turning me on. It was watching *him* give them to her. I tried to focus, to keep my mind on the fact that this was all for Carlie, but it was an impossible feat.

The little suction noises he was making. The way Carlie turned her face into my neck and whimpered. The sight of his stubble, wet from her pussy. It was sensory overload. I had to fuck her, immediately.

"Stop," I grated out, my voice sounding harsh to my own ears. "Strip, and sit over there."

I moved my chin, directing Zach to sit on the sofa. He stopped instantly and looked up at me. Eyes narrowing like he was trying to guess my plans.

I couldn't tear my eyes away from him as he lifted his t-shirt over his head. His abs twisted and contracted with the movement. Why was that so sexy? I had no attraction to men. None.

At least...I didn't think I did.

He smirked like he could hear my internal thoughts as his hands moved to his joggers. Slowly, he slid them down over his hips and I swallowed as he stood, tall, proud...and hard.

Carlie sucked in a breath, "Oh my god..."

Yeah.

Zach stalked over to the sofa and sat down, spreading his legs wide and arching his eyebrow, silently allowing me to continue. I pushed in between Carlie's shoulders so she bent at the waist and put her hands on his knees.

"Suck him, Carlie. Show him what you can do with that beautiful mouth of yours," I demanded.

Before she could take him, I shrugged my trousers to my ankles and thrust into her. She screamed in pleasure, her voice echoing in the room. The feeling of her tight, slick cunt surrounding my cock sent me spiralling.

"Fucking suck him, Carlie, now!"

His head fell back as she took Zach's cock in her mouth. We were the perfect vision of debauchery. It was everything I shouldn't want, and everything I never knew I needed. His groans of arousal spurred me on. Carlie needed to go first though. His fist gripped her hair and I pinched her clit causing her to pull her mouth away and she fell forward.

"Fuck her harder, Blake. Let me hear those screams I've been dreaming of. I bet her greedy cunt is so tight. I want inside, so fuck her like you have a point to prove."

Zach's words made my blood heat, and not in anger. Pure lust shot through my veins and my hips punched forward. My breaths came in short pants and the heat radiating from my cock pushed me closer to orgasm. The smell of sex permeated the air around us as Zach slid out from underneath Carlie and stood from the sofa. My thrusts faltered when he moved to stand behind me.

His breath washed over my skin and goose bumps broke out along my neck, "Are you listening, Blake? Hear how close she is?" He licked a path from my shoulder to my ear, "I bet she's drenched. Look at how flushed her skin is. You're her husband, Blake, give her what she needs."

I wasn't sure how to feel when he smoothed his hand from my shoulder, along my arm and moved my hand with his, around Carlie's hip and circled her clit with my fingers but my pulse skyrocketed.

"Blake, Zach, Blake..." She moaned incoherently.

Her legs shook, her hands gripped the cushion in an iron grip and she threw her head back, screaming my name into the room as her pussy clamped down and she came harder than I'd ever seen. Falling forward onto the sofa, I missed her heat instantly as my shaft slipped free. Before I could get my bearings, Zach moved to his knees, took my cock in his mouth and sucked deep.

I wanted to protest. I wanted to refuse.

But his mouth was like a suction furnace and I growled, driving my fingers into the short strands of his hair and pulling him deeper. His eyes were on mine, mine were on his and I couldn't look away. The stubble on his cheeks against my thighs, driving me insane every time he sucked me into his mouth.

Never, not *ever*, had it ever felt so good.

His fingers grabbed my ass and pushed my hips forward, taking my cock fully into his throat.

"Fuck! I'm going to come," I warned.

His grin was wicked, he wanted it. He massaged my balls in his palm, tugging lightly and tipping me over the edge. I held his head in a firm grasp and thrust my throbbing shaft deep, watching as his throat worked to swallow my cum.

Sitting back on his heels; he licked his lips, winked, and moved to Carlie.

My brain whirled. What the fuck did I do?

And more importantly...

Why did it feel like the best thing that ever happened to me?

CHAPTER

Seven

Minutes after 'the incident' a few days before, Zach had stood, shrugged on his clothes and kissed Carlie on the forehead as he left our house. No one had spoken a single word. The house had been silent, only the sounds of breathing filled the room. I was lost in my head but I still didn't know what everyone else's thoughts were because I couldn't bring myself to ask.

I'd had the most incredible sex of my life with Carlie, but then let a *man* blow me until I came in his mouth. Had Carlie watched? Did she like it? Again, I hadn't asked and she hadn't mentioned it.

She seemed, I don't know, normal. Or normal by her standards anyway. Outwardly, to her, it was like nothing had ever happened. For me, on the other hand, I couldn't stop thinking about it. The whole night was playing on repeat in my mind and in my dreams. I woke up in a cold sweat with my cock hard as steel and seconds away from coming.

But I wasn't dreaming of Carlie.

I was dreaming of Zach on his knees, Zach in my bed, and Zach's hands on my body.

And I was rapidly driving myself to the point of

insanity with it.

I didn't want to be dreaming of *any* man, let alone him.

I forced myself to work and to concentrate, praying that my wayward thoughts were just a phase. A leftover consequence of delving deeper into the world of sexual exploration. I needed the phase to pass, and quickly. I needed it gone from my mind. I had a new job to learn, a marriage to save and a life to repair. I couldn't do that with thoughts of someone else filling my brain.

I arrived home after a long, stressful day at the station. It was always dull when the team was out all day and since my job had changed and I had to stay in the office, it was worse. In a strange way though, that was when I felt most at home. When I was there on my own and I could just...be.

Home was a different matter. I was still walking on eggshells, waiting for Carlie to come up with another crazy scheme or idea that was going to make my head explode. She was able to be, capable of being, and used to be, a lively, sweet and *rational* person.

I just needed to bring that Carlie back.

So when I walked into the lounge to find her sitting there, wearing nothing but one of my shirts, buttons undone. Her heels up on the sofa, knees bent, legs slightly parted and her pink, plump pussy on display, I froze.

"You're on time," she noted, needlessly. She was running a tiny pink bullet vibrator lightly against her folds. "I want to play again."

I dropped my bag, undid my belt and kicked my trousers off. My shirt followed, then my socks and my boxers. I stood before her, completely naked and watched her face as her eyes moved over my body. The draft from the open window sent goose bumps crawling along my skin and I shivered but my cock jumped. I wanted inside her pussy something fierce.

The need was unbearable.

But wrong.

I wanted to be inside her because I needed to prove to myself that I *could* do it. Not because I actually wanted to make love to my wife. The thought ratcheted my pulse sky high. This was a necessary thing I had to do.

Imperative.

And all that shot to shit when she next spoke.

"I text Zach. He's free. He wants in. He'll be here in about thirty seconds and tonight *I'm* the one in charge."

My heart thumped.

How could she do that to me?

"You can't just..."

"I can. It's done. You turn him away and I'll walk myself upstairs, pack a bag and go stay somewhere else until you get your head out of your ass. I want this. He wants this. And *you* want this. You just won't admit it as easily as we will. I want him in my pussy and I want you in my ass. We've done it before with my toys, it feels good. I'm going to pass out from pleasure when I'm so full of cock that I can feel you *both* in my throat," I stopped breathing. "I love the feel of you, Blake. Call me greedy but I want the feel of him too. I want to watch his face as *your* balls slap against his when you're both pounding into me. I want to feel him thrust in as you pull out and I want to feel you both come so deep inside me, that I'm walking around with you both dripping out of me for days."

My lungs wouldn't work.

Instead of thinking about all the things *she* wanted, I thought about what I wanted and realised that there was no denying it. Her words had sent shockwaves rippling through my cock and when the doorbell rang, I admitted to myself that I wanted it to. *Exactly* as she had described it.

I craved every detail.

Including the ones she hadn't verbalised.

I wanted to feel her ass tighten around my cock. I wanted to hear her screams of pleasure as she had two guys hammering in and out of her holes. I wanted to watch as she bounced on Zach's cock and in turn, bounced on mine. I wanted it all. Including him. I wanted to watch as he filled her, as his balls slapped against mine, as he emptied himself her pussy.

I wanted to watch *him*.

So I opened the door. Naked. Hard. Ready.

His eyes dropped to my cock but he showed no reaction. He pushed his way inside, squeezing the head of my cock lightly on the way past and making me whimper. Carlie heard it. Her eyes flared. She liked it. In fact, she *loved* it when he touched me. I wouldn't admit that I did too but I could play that part. I could give her that fantasy, and I would.

Zach's trousers hit the floor as he moved further into the room, his ass flexing with each step. Before he could remove his shirt, Carlie said, "Stop!"

And he stopped.

"Leave the shirt, I want you to stand there and I want to watch you touch yourself."

His hand grabbed his cock in a firm gripped and he stroked. He grew, he stretched and he thickened as she watched. I watched too because I had no choice, my eyes were fixated. My own manhood throbbed and I reached down, squeezing at the root and pressing in roughly. I needed it to slow down. I needed time.

"Carlie..." I growled in warning.

She could not sit like that, spit those words and leave her pussy on display the second I get home and then make me wait to be inside her. It was an impossible task if she was thinking that I had the patience to see this through if we were playing games. I just wanted to fuck her, I wanted him to fuck her. I wanted it hard, rough, and uncontrollable. And I wanted *instantly.*

Her lips twitched.

"Is my poor baby getting desperate?" She crooned.

"I don't want to talk and I don't want to wait. I just want to fuck. Sit his ass down, straddle his hips and take him inside. I want to see him take you. I want to watch your tits bounce in his face and his mouth suck your nipples deep before I force my cock inside your ass and prove who you really belong to."

Zach choked on a breath and Carlie sunk two fingers inside her cunt at my words. She moaned.

"Do it, Zach. She wanted to be in charge but she fucked that chance because she waited. This isn't a fucking tète a tète, you're here to fuck and we're going to do it. So sit your ass down, spread your legs and let her ride you," I demanded, my voice cutting through the rivers of lust flowing through the room.

He sat his ass down, she scrambled on top, facing him and impaled herself on his cock. Her head flew back and her eyes hit mine over her shoulder.

"God Zach," she groaned. "You're so fucking big. Filling me, stretching me."

Even when she was getting what she wanted, she had to play games. Her attempts at making me jealous didn't work. They didn't make feel jealous, they made me feel the force of wrath sear through me.

She was acting like a bitch. Bouncing on his cock, his fingers digging into her hips as she rode him. But she was waiting for *me* to react to her fucking another man. It wasn't going to happen. Watching her ass bounce, her tits jiggle and *his* face while she did it. My dick felt like an iron fist and she was going to regret trying playing games with my head.

I met Zach's eyes, his desire burning in their depths. He leaned forward, sucking one of Carlie's nipples deep into his mouth. She gasped and he grinned as he bit down, tugging her sensitive skin with his teeth. He listened. He knew when I'd give in and join them because he'd *listened*. Carlie hadn't.

I know she hadn't because she wasn't prepared when I spat in my hand, stroked my cock, wetting it, and slid in between Zach's open thighs. Carlie's fingers were on his shoulders and she had her eyes closed in the throes of ecstasy. Zach stopped moving his hips, her eyes flew open and she frowned down at him, not paying attention to me.

So when I thrust forward, spearing her ass open with my cock. She screamed, tears pricked her eyes and her noises fell to a whimper. I didn't stop, she wanted it, she begged for it and she'd take it all.

Carlie cried, "¡Joder! Duele tan bien!" *Fuck! It hurts so good!*

"Montarlo, bebé," Zach replied, making my heart stop beating. "Sienta que. Coño puta codicioso. Eres tan llena de polla. Coño y culo. Teniendo todo. Mendigar para él. ¿Te gusta ser una puta sucia,

Carlie? Eres jodidamente empapados. Apretando mi polla. Puedo sentir a tu esposo en el culo. Sentir sus bolas acariciando a mina. ¿Que quieres, no te Carlie? Quiere sentirlo también."

Ride it, baby. Feel it. Greedy fucking cunt. You're so full of cock. Pussy and ass. Taking it all. Begging for it. Do you like being a dirty whore, Carlie? You're fucking drenched. Squeezing my cock. I can feel your husband moving in your ass. Feel his balls stroking mine. You want that, don't you Carlie? You want me to feel him too.

Oh fuck!

It was *his* voice, in that language. No idea whatsoever what he said but the dark rasp of his voice made it sound deliciously filthy.

I couldn't deal with it.

It took a second, two, and Carlie's head fell forward onto Zach's shoulder. Biting down, she tried to muffle her moans but the pressure was too much, she felt too full. Her hips moved, shifting backwards and forwards. Full of him, then full of me. She couldn't get enough.

Zach's gaze didn't move from my face but I felt it *everywhere*.

The way I felt, it was as if he could have been sticking his dick into anything and any*one* but he still would have been right there, with me, doing it *for* me. His look scorched me, claimed me and branded me, but I didn't understand it. I wasn't ready to mentally dissect it either.

We moved in sync. He thrust, then I thrust. He moved, then I moved.

Carlie screamed in pleasure with every single inch. Every touch, every noise, every breath, she was feeling it.

Pleasure overload.

We caused that. Me and Zach. We gave that to her. I gave that to him and he gave it to me.

I sunk my teeth into the skin between Carlie's neck and shoulder, sucking hard enough to mark her. To give her something tender, an ache, that she would walk around with for days or weeks afterwards and be brought right back to that moment.

That moment, being when my control snapped and I put my hands above Zach's on her hips and yanked her ass back at the same time as I punched my hips forward. Every inch of my swollen cock was buried in her tight little asshole, she was squeezing and clenching around me. I felt the first ripple of her orgasm build in her ass and as she finally let go and dived into the depths of desire, I pulled out.

The effect was instant.

She cried out, slamming her hips down onto Zach's dick and arching her back. She went boneless in his grasp, shaking, quivering and completely incoherent as fluid flowed from her pussy, coating Zach's skin and making his eyes roll back.

I moved.

"Suck me. Do it fast. Put your mouth on my cock and drain me," I growled, eyes on Zach.

He leaned forward, moving Carlie to one side and he sucked me into his mouth. It was wet, hot and I felt my cum building. Carlie watched. Her eyes still glassy and her chest still heaving for breath, she edged forward too. Flicking her gaze to Zach's mouth on my cock, then to my eyes and back again.

Sated, spent and well fucked she looked every inch the wanton little whore that she wanted to pretend she was.

And she proved it. When she leaned forward,

matching Zach's position and wrapped her fingers around my balls, twisting and massaging. She opened her mouth and took them in.

Zach's mouth sucking deep on my cock, Carlie's holding and pleasuring my balls.

I exploded.

My knees shook, my fingers ached and my balls tightened in Carlie's mouth as my cum shot from my shaft, to the back of Zach's throat and he swallowed every drop.

I left. I walked to the stairs and jogged up. I tried to ignore the feel of my cock, wet from Zach's mouth and my cum, hitting against my thigh. I locked the bathroom door, not caring what they were doing downstairs.

I leant back against the door, but faced the bathroom mirror.

Then I laughed humourlessly, not knowing who the person was staring back at me.

"Blake Thomas," I shook my head. "You are *so* fucked."

CHAPTER
Eight

Three days later, I found myself outside Pro-Weight's gym and I had no idea how I'd come to be there. My head was a mess and I was living in a daze.

And that was why I stood on the pavement outside the gym that Zach owned. Though I still hadn't decided what exactly I was there to say. Before I could talk myself out of it, I swung the door open and stepped inside. The smell of stale sweat masked with bleach filled my senses. How Carlie could stand to spend time there, I would never understand.

I froze in the doorway and the receptionist looked up at me with a false smile.

"Good Morning, can I help you?"

"I, um."

She frowned at me, "Are you ok?"

"No, I," words failed me.

"Maria, can you pull up all the expired records and make a list of names please? If you pass them on to Nyle, he's organising all the details for the membership drive," Zach's voice echoed across the foyer and the receptionist looked over to the left.

"Sure, Zach. No problem," she gave him a megawatt smile and fluttered her eyelashes.

Wherever Zach came from, he disappeared again seconds later.

In the silence that followed, my heart rate escalated and my palms began to sweat. My reaction was ridiculous and I wanted to kick myself for not being able to pull myself together. The talk I needed to have with him wasn't going to go the way I wanted it to if I couldn't even focus enough to speak.

"Sir, seriously, do you need something?" Maria addressed me but she was clearly edging towards impatience.

"Zach," I managed to spit out.

"You need to speak to Zach? Would you like me to call him?"

"Yes," I demanded, unable to say any more.

She gave me an odd look but pressed a button on her desk. Zach answered through the speaker.

"There is someone in reception who wishes to speak to you," Maria told him, glancing back up at me.

"Does this someone have a name?"

She raised her eyebrows but I shook my head, I couldn't take the risk that he'd avoid me.

"He says no, he doesn't have a name."

Zach sighed and the speaker clicked off.

"He'll be right with you," Maria advised before going back to her computer.

Appearing from the corridor, he paused and his eyes widened. His steps slowed as he approached.

"Blake."

I sucked in a breath through my nose. Whatever was going on in my brain, he was the solution, I just needed to find out why, and how.

"I need to talk to you," I explained.

"Here? Or do we need to go to my office?"

For reasons unknown to me, my heart faltered in my chest. The thought of being alone with him behind closed doors both excited and terrified me all at once. Talking out in the open wasn't an option though.

"Office," I decided.

Without word, he turned on his heel and tilted his head for me to follow. We stepped inside and he closed the door behind me and the click of the lock sounded. I wasted a few seconds to look around the room without taking anything in. I felt like the walls were closing in on me and there wasn't enough air. I jumped when Zach spoke, not realising he was so close to me.

"So what can I do for you, Blake? You look like you're about to pass out."

"I want to know why you did it," I started. "I need to know why you did *that* to me. The first time."

"What exactly is *that* that you're referring to?" He asked, knowing full well what I meant.

"Don't make this difficult for me, Zach."

Leaning into my face, his mouth was so close to mine and I fought the urge to flinch away, "Are you referring to the fact that I dropped to my knees and sucked your dick until you came like a racehorse in my mouth and then swallowed every drop?"

That time, I did flinch, "Jesus."

"What about it?"

"Why did you do that?" I asked.

He shrugged, "Do you have *any* idea how hard my dick was by then? How much I wanted to feel you on me, in me, surrounding me? Blake, I fuck women, I fuck men, but only one of them ever really gets me off. Want to take a wild guess as to who does it for me considering I've been with you and Carlie twice now, yet I haven't cum once?" Without letting me answer, he carried on. "The whole time Carlie was giving head like a rock star, going for it with all she had, I was looking at you. Wishing it was your mouth on me. I had two choices, give you a mind-blowing orgasm, or bend over and beg you to fuck me. We both know I made the right choice and I don't regret a second. If you're honest with yourself, you don't either. If you did, you wouldn't have let it happen a second time and you definitely wouldn't have demanded that I suck your cock again. You might not like your thoughts now, but you wouldn't be here right now if you were able to stop thinking about it."

Well, shit.

There was a lot to sort through and not enough time, or space, to do it.

"I'm not gay and I'm fucking married," I reminded him heatedly.

He smirked, "You don't have to be gay to like getting your dick sucked, Blake. And in case you've already forgotten, it was *your wife* who invited me to your little sexual adventure."

"Well I haven't forgotten that detail," I muttered.

"You still haven't said why you're here, Blake. I'm starting to think you don't even know the answer to that yourself."

"No, no, I do. I'm here because, because, I'm here to tell you that it will never happen again," I confirmed with a nod.

"Right," he said slowly. "I haven't spoken to you, or Carlie, since the other night. Again, it was *your wife* who asked for it *both* times. I haven't tried to contact either of you and I never said anything about wanting more. So again, why are you really here?"

"Because!" I exploded, standing taller and fisting

my hands. "I don't fucking know, ok! I don't know. It wasn't supposed to be like that and I wasn't supposed to feel like this. You, you're...you're a fucking *man*, for fuck sake! What happened, that's not ok. You've played with my head and I don't know why or how, but you just need to, to," I ran my hands roughly through my hair and growled in frustration. "You just need to fuck off, Zach. It's not ok for you to play with people's lives like this."

And it wasn't ok. His hold was like a prison cell that I couldn't escape from. Metaphorically speaking of course.

He huffed out a laugh and crossed his arms, still not moving away from me.

"You loved it. Don't come here, to my gym, to my office and start spouting shit at me because you can't handle how you feel. It's not my fault you're only just opening your eyes. It's not my fault that you've been living under a cloud. You don't know a single fucking thing about me, Blake. But I know you and I knew everything there was to know before I even met you. It's not even the thought of what happened that's confusing you so much, it's the thought that you *know* you want it to happen again and again."

"That's not, it's not," I stuttered, both in fear and in denial of his words.

My pulse increased and my breathing faltered when Zach stepped closer, his hand brushed my thigh and I froze. Did I want him touching me? Even I didn't personally know the answer to that question. My body seemed to react, my brain had already fled the vicinity.

"You're already lying and you haven't even finished your thought," he accused. "Admit it, Blake. You want me, in every way, and you just don't know how to handle that."

I stayed silent.

He whispered, "Admit it," again.

And I caved.

I fused my mouth against his, kissing him with intensity, with a need I'd never known. The feeling was...strange. But in a really, really good way. My blood roared in my ears and any rational thoughts fled. Thirty-five years old and the best kiss I'd ever had, was my first kiss with Zach. A man.

"You want this," Zach said as he pulled back. A question disguised in a statement.

I shook my head, not realising what I was going to say until I said it, "I need this."

"Tell me you won't hate me, or blame me, for what happens next," he demanded.

At that, I paused. I watched him, watching me. He needed that from me, he needed to know that I wouldn't make him carry the guilt of whatever happened. Could I do it? I didn't have a choice. In the back of my mind, the sensible part of me was clawing its way forward telling me that this wasn't a new and exciting adventure. It was cheating. Pure and simple. Worse, it was cheating with a man. It was official, I was the worst husband.

"Stop thinking so much. Are we going to do this?"

"We're going to do this," I confirmed, not hesitating any longer with my answer. Mind made up, I knew that was the reason I had turned up to see Zach in the first place and it was the only way I was going to get my answers. Maybe it was just the new experience that was messing with my head, or maybe it was Zach. I was about to find out.

Zach ran his hand across my jaw, "You're nervous."

His statement didn't need a response, but I nodded anyway, "Terrified."

I couldn't lie to him, I felt it written all over my face. Who wouldn't be nervous? Scared?

His hand dropped to the waistband of my trousers and slid inside. The sensation of his rough skin against my cock sent all my blood rushing south. It should have felt wrong.

It didn't.

It felt fucking amazing.

Whispering his words against my ear, he made my aching cock throb in his grasp, "You're already hard for me, Blake. All that anger is misdirected. You need to let it out, I know, but it's about actions, not words. You need this, you need *me* to take it from you. I'll fuck you with my hand, my mouth and my tongue. Don't think, just feel."

Thoughts? I had no idea what they were. It was all about touch, about taste and smell.

"Kiss me," he prompted.

He didn't miss a beat, his tongue danced with mine as his hand sped up the glide of his palm against my shaft. My conscience was screaming at me but I couldn't hear the words over the sounds of my own breathing. My trousers fell to my feet and Zach looked down, biting his lip.

"Lean back."

I leaned back against the office door, feet parted, arms flat against the frame. He sunk to his knees in front of me and in that moment, it hit me like a freight train. *That* was what I'd been craving. *That* was what I hadn't been able to get out of my mind. The image of this broad, proud, sculpted man, on his knees in front of me. My cock jumped in front of him, even if my mind wasn't one hundred percent sure that I should be doing it, my little brain clearly was.

"Suck me, Zach, please," I begged, tired of holding back.

He licked the head of my cock and teased the length causing my thighs to tense, "Don't tease me."

He sucked deep but chuckled under his breath at the same time and fuck if that didn't feel incredible. The vibrations of his laughter shot through my shaft and the heated lust curled in my stomach. My head swung backwards, hitting the door with a thud but the pain didn't register. Zach hardened his tongue and only used the tip. Somehow, though I would have thought it was impossible, my pleasure soared. I moaned his name and closed my eyes, I couldn't watch anymore. I felt his hand grip my ass but I clenched my muscles when his fingers ran in between my cheeks. I wouldn't cope with whatever he had planned.

"Relax for me, Blake," his words were merely a whisper, but I felt them flow through me like he'd screamed them. "I promise I'll make it good for you. Let me own all of this."

I forced myself to relax. His finger eased closer to that forbidden tight ring of muscle and I swallowed audibly.

My cock slid free from his mouth and I almost whimpered, I needed him back.

"Hold on to the door frame," I hesitated so he moved head further away from where I wanted him. "Do it. Hold on."

My hands curled around the edge of the door frame and my knuckles turned white. The second I had a firm grip, he sucked my cock to the back of his throat and pushed one finger beyond my limits. The pain I was expecting didn't come. The intense burn was the match that ignited my lust, "Fuck!"

He moved it slowly, edging in and out of my hole in sync with his mouth. My orgasm didn't build, it destroyed. Frozen in place, I squeezed my eyelids together and clung to the door frame as the pleasure ripped through me, leaving my body devastated and liquid. Zach soothed his hand against my thigh, waiting for my breathing to calm.

"Respira, Blake," he whispered. "No hay nada mejor en este mundo, que el sabor de su orgasmo."

Breath, Blake. There is nothing better in this world, than the taste of your orgasm.

Unable to hold myself up anymore, I slid down the wall, bending my knees and collapsing on to the sterile tile floor.

"Fuck," I cursed. "How...how..."

I stuttered, not able to form the question I needed to ask. He knew what I was trying to say.

"Because the way to reacted to Carlie's foreign words the other night and the way you reacted to mine. It's your trigger, it makes you weak in the knees," he shrugged one shoulder. "I was brought up using both languages because my dad used to own a place out in Mallorca."

A glimpse into his life. Something that I wasn't sure I wanted but it somehow felt good to know. Ridiculous. Fucked up. My mind was more jumbled than before.

I would never be the same, I felt it in my soul.

I managed to drag myself off the floor and fasten the buttons on my trousers when his hand came to the back of my head and he forced my eyes away from the floor, to him.

The man was an enigma. So confident, so cocky, so damn egotistical.

Yet, soft. His movements, the way he touched, the way he protected. A contradiction. A puzzle that I somehow knew I would have to figure out.

"Don't overthink things. It is what it is and we both enjoyed it. Go home, Blake. Go home to your wife and life just goes on. Simple," I nodded at him and turned to leave. With my hand on the doorknob, he called, "Oh, but, Blake?"

I looked back over my shoulder to see his eyes darken and he grinned.

"Next time, it's my turn."

Seeing the lust in his eyes, I sucked in a breath and took a second to think about how I'd feel with that. I realised that the idea turned me on a lot more than it should. Life was getting complicated. Zach smiled and flicked his hand to the door, probably knowing that I needed to escape. So I fled the building, ignoring the receptionist's look of knowing, and headed back to the station.

I may have escaped his presence physically.

But with the way his lust filled gaze was with me every which way I turned, I couldn't escape him in my mind.

He was a mistake. More than a mistake.

Yet it felt like the best mistake I'd ever made.

CHAPTER
Nine

I returned home just before seven, after taking a shower back at the station.

If anything, I was feeling more confused and shaken than I had been hours before. I was certain that I would walk through the front door and be bombarded with accusations and insults. That didn't happen. In fact, nothing did. Carlie was curled up asleep on the sofa, her knees tucked to her chest and her head rested on one hand.

I pulled the blanket from the back and laid it over her, smiling when she mumbled in her sleep.

Then I paused.

When did I become the sort of person that would cheat on his wife? How could I pretend?

I felt sick at my actions. I never claimed to be the best liar but I was convinced that I could hide it from her until the day I died. I made my mind up. My fascination with Zach was just that, a fascination. It was done with. I couldn't hurt Carlie like that, even if I already had.

Then Zach's whispered vow before I left his office filtered through my brain and I couldn't clear it from my mind. Repeating, over and over and over.

Next time, it's my turn.

Next time. He wasn't joking, and he wasn't saying

it like a suggestion. It was a stone vow. Like he was one hundred percent sure that there would be a next time and from the heat in his eyes I knew he was already thinking about it.

Admittedly...so was I.

An endless cycle of pornographic images, plaguing my thoughts.

I couldn't live like that.

Scrubbing my hands roughly across my face, I sighed in confusion. I needed time to think and space away from everything. My life had turned upside down in the span of a couple of weeks, yet I seemed to have no control over it. My actions were unforgivable, but unpreventable. I didn't make the choice to go to Zach. I didn't make the choice to watch with passion and desire clouding my vision, as he tongued my cock and made me come. The decision was made for me and I was driven by a force that I couldn't understand.

It wasn't natural. But it also didn't feel altogether *unnatural* either.

A mind-fuck.

Bringing myself back to reality, I stroked Carlie's forehead, pushing her hair to one side.

"Carlie? Honey, wake up," I coaxed, waiting until her eyes blinked open. "Get yourself off to bed, you'll get neck ache sleeping like that."

Her eyes flicked around the room for a few beats like she couldn't remember where she was, then she blinked and smiled through a yawn.

"Hey! How long have you been home?"

"Not long, have you eaten?" She shook her head.

"Alright, want me to order in? Chinese? Pizza?"

Her lips pursed. Between the gym and her obsession with looking incredible, she wasn't a huge fan of takeaway food, or any high-calorie food at all. It had always been that way. Honestly, I thought it was something she would just ease up about as she got older, but if anything, it had been getting worse.

"One Chow Mein isn't going to kill you, Carlie. Hell, let's go wild, I'll order some chicken rolls and prawn crackers while I'm at it," I joked. Her face went pale. "Bloody hell, I'm getting food. If you want to go eat rabbit food then I'm not going to stop you."

I hadn't meant to snap at her but I'd been saying for months that she needed to see a therapist or something. It wasn't an eating disorder as such because she was healthy and she did eat. It was just an obsession with being perfect. I googled it once and convinced myself that she had body dysmorphia. Turns out, it's not the best idea to tell her that though. I think that was the one time I've ever been genuinely a little terrified of my own wife.

The food came half an hour later. Carlie hadn't spoken to me but I'd ordered enough for her anyway. I laid the cartons out on the table and starting picking at the noodles. I suddenly felt like my stomach was tied in knots and couldn't force the food down fast enough. Something that should be a normal, essential everyday task like eating; felt like it was taking all my strength.

I stacked the half-empty containers on the work surface, not bothering to clean up properly and stalked up the stairs. I just wanted to crawl into bed and forget the day ever happened.

Funny how the second I lay down, memories assaulted my brain.

I closed my eyes and let the visions play out. Zach on his knees, the feel of his tongue in my mouth, the way he ran his fingers across my chin, the smell of his aftershave filling my senses. My cock jumped and I stifled a groan. Carlie shuffled closer to me and wrapped her arm around my waist. I bent one leg at the knee to hide my stiffening member. I wouldn't be able to make love to my wife with the thoughts of another person in my head.

It was so, so wrong.

My phone buzzed on the bedside table, an unknown number.

"Your cock. My mouth. Have you managed to stop thinking about it yet?"

I quickly shut it down and threw it back, praying Carlie hadn't seen anything.

Was it just a fascination?

Because with the way my palms were sweating and my fingers were trembling, I felt like an addict. Like I was having withdrawal symptoms from a man I'd known less than two weeks, and who I'd only *had*, three times.

"I love you, Blake," Carlie whispered in the darkness.

"Te quiero, Carlie," I replied, using one of the only phrases I knew.

And I wasn't lying. I did love her. It was quickly becoming apparent to though, that maybe I wasn't *in* love with her anymore. I just wished I knew what to do about it or how to fix it.

The bed sheets felt too rough on my skin, Carlie felt too warm and clammy against me. I gave up on staying in our bed, and stomped back down the stairs like an angry bull. I pulled the blanket over me on the sofa and closed my eyes.

Fuck Zack and his ability to invade my life.

I would never give up on my marriage or my wife, even if my heart already had already begun to switch off. Couples fight through problems every day and come out stronger, I wanted that to happen with us.

My final thought as I drifted off to sleep was that, if I could convince myself I was being honest, maybe I could convince the rest of the world too.

Somehow, it didn't feel as easy as it sounded.

Morning came before I was ready for it. Carlie had already gone, leaving a note on the lounge table about hitting the gym before work. I scowled, then rolled my eyes at my own actions. Being jealous that she was at the one place I could never go again was ridiculous and it was *those* thoughts that I was going to have to battle.

By the time I got to work, I was feeling ready to take on the day. I was a thirty-five year old man for fuck sake and it was time I started acting like it. No more. I'd had multiple texts from Carlie throughout the morning, just checking in. It was something she never did before, but it felt...I don't know, necessary, that day for some unknown reason.

My office walls actually seemed like they were cocooning me. Keeping me safe inside from anything that was willing to attempt to get in. The thought was ridiculous, but it was there all the same. It felt like a dark day. Like yet *another* something that I couldn't control was about to happen. So yeah, my office became my safe place to hide from the rest of the world.

Until it wasn't anymore

"Hey, Bossman?" Marc poked his head around the office door a few hours later.

"What's up?" I asked.

"I was just wondering if it's alright for me to take a longer lunch today."

Considering we had a canteen at the station, they

only had half an hour and the guys didn't usually leave the building for lunch, it was an odd request. I frowned.

"Why? I mean, as long as you're back within an hour then I don't have a problem with it, but why?"

He actually blushed and if he hadn't look so nervous, I would have made some comment about him needing to grow a pair. Ha! Like I could talk. Pot, meet kettle, it's black.

"I'm meeting my girl's sister in town. I'm going to ask her to marry me, so I wanted her help choosing the ring," he explained.

"You're going to ask your girl's sister to marry you?" I teased.

"What? No, no! I just meant..."

His stuttering made me take pity on him and I interrupted him with a laugh, "I know what you meant. It's no problem you can..."

The printer in the main room clicked and started to print, setting everyone in action. The tip-sheet came through and the sirens blared. Everyone threw their cards down from the game they'd been playing and immediately started suiting up.

I turned to Marc, who was already six feet away, moving towards his locker. I stood back and watched, ignoring that familiar pang in my chest that happened every time they left without me.

The dispatcher started to speak.

"All engines required. Large building fire, Pro-Weight's gym. Multiple persons suspected to be inside," squawked across the tannoy. "Code blue. Urgent response required, stat."

"Guess shopping will have to wait, Marc," he waved me off. That's the thing about the job, when you're needed, nothing else matters.

Then my heart just stopped beating, grabbing hold of the person nearest to me as he walked past, his face blurred as I attempted to hold myself up, "Did that say Pro-Weight's gym?"

Matt's concerned face came into view, "Yeah. Are you alright?"

Without thought, I scrambled towards my locker and grabbed my gear, throwing it on and suiting up within milliseconds. My body was on autopilot, my brain switched to protection mode.

"Blake!" Matt called.

"This is all hands on deck, guys. You're going to need everyone, that includes me," I explained, which was actually true, regardless of the fact that my insides were crippled with panic.

Within seconds, we were packed into the engines and racing towards our target. My hands were trembling and I knew more than one of the guys had noticed. Their faces were worried, and not about the fire, that was their job. No, that worry was all about my reaction. I had to pull myself together quickly before my nerves affected my job.

I could smell the smoke before I saw the building, it was a hauntingly familiar smell. For the first time in my life, I had a *personal* reason to be there and that should have been my first warning that I was doing the wrong thing. I quickly scanned the waiting faces, some openly shocked, some weirdly curious...all of them were worried.

None of them were Zach.

Seeing as I was the highest ranked there, I started barking orders as soon as the engine stopped.

"Matt, Marc, you two take the ladders and see if you can get in anywhere up there," I pointed to the broken fire escape. "Dave, you come with me and we'll go in from the back and see if we can get anyone out through there. Harry, man the hose and be on alert in case engine two needs you."

I didn't stop to check if they understood, this wasn't our first rodeo. I launched myself from the vehicle and pushed my legs to fight through my sudden onset of nerves. Smoke billowed from the roof of the building and I could see the flames dancing through open windows on the top floor. Never a good sign.

The back door gave way easily under a swift kick to the lock. I shook my head, yet another reason to kick Zach's ass when I saw him again. *If* I ever saw him alive again.

Fuck. My heart spasmed in my chest.

The smoke was thick, but the heat wasn't too bad which told me two things. The good, the fire was far enough away from that part of the building, we had enough time to get people out. The bad, it was burning bad enough elsewhere that no one would survive the smoke inhalation anywhere close to it.

Not wanting to waste any time, I shouted over to Dave, "You take those two side rooms, I'll see if there's any access up those stairs."

"Boss?" I knew why he was questioning me, we didn't split up, but damn it! Someone I cared about was inside that building and I wasn't waiting around.

Losing my temper, I snapped at him.

"Just fucking do it!" And as an afterthought, "but be careful!"

With a split-second hesitation, he moved and I made my way towards the stairs. A flickering orange glow kissing the top step told me I was getting close, too close. I was screaming Zach's name under my mask, praying that he wasn't hurt. My eyes took a few beats to adjust to the darkness of the top floor, the torch on my helmet barely helping at all through the smoke. The heat became almost unbearable and I could feel the sweat pouring down my forehead.

Voices drifted through my earpiece, letting everyone know that two women had been rescued from the upstairs bathroom.

"Do we have reports on anyone left in here?" I screamed into the mic.

"Conflicting reports, Boss. Witnesses say the owner was still inside but the receptionist said he wasn't supposed to be in. We have people searching, get yourself out of there now, the place isn't secure."

"I'll take the top floor for the search. Get everyone else out," I replied, still moving around the edges of the floor.

"Boss, we have this covered, get out!"

Ignoring the voices, I carried on. My gut was burning with fear but that annoying voice in my head kept telling me I had to do this. I *had* to find Zach. I had something to prove to myself, to others. I needed to know, in my heart, that I was still capable of doing the job. My throat was starting to ache from calling Zach's name but I doubted he could hear me over the roaring of the fire.

The smoke was too thick, the heat too strong, no one could survive it without the proper equipment.

"Blake, get out of there, *now!*"

Again, I ignored their warnings.

"You stubborn, stupid, asshole. We need to retreat. It's not fucking *safe!*"

"Do we have everyone out?" I growled, refusing to give in until I knew the building was clear. It might have been about Zach for me, but they didn't know that. It was my job for god sake. No matter who or what was inside, I wouldn't have given up until I knew we wouldn't be losing lives. I lived and breathed for it.

"Matt, Dave, status?"

"Bottom floor is clear, I'm coming out," Dave replied, then, "I've circled the top floor, anywhere accessible is clear. I'm already out." Matt.

It gave me a moment's reprieve, knowing at least, that my team was out. In one last ditch attempt to find Zach, I ripped off my oxygen mask and screamed his name. My voice gave out under the strain and morphed into a gut-clenched cough, my entire upper body heaved with each breath.

It's in those moments, that split second, when you realise that you've gone from being in danger, to being in *imminent* danger.

Trust me, there's a monumental difference.

The instant pain in my lungs told me I'd be laid up for a while at minimum. Not good. The creaking of the foundations around me told me I'd be lucky to even make it that long. *Really* not good.

"I'm coming out," I croaked through the mic. Putting my mask back over my face, for all the good it was going to do at that point, I took one last lingering look around the devastated building. I knew in my gut that I'd done all I could, it still didn't seem enough.

I made my way down the stairs, the flames licking at my back, the rumble of falling debris filling my ears. My lungs burned with every intake of breathe and my head started to spin. Legs almost giving way, I couldn't have been more relieved to see the rage-filled face of my colleague, Matt, at the bottom.

"Crazy, stupid motherfucker. Let's move before

this whole fucking place goes down!"

He grabbed my arm and swung it around his shoulders, supporting my weight. It took seconds to reach the back door, most of the lower level already saturated, just black smoke and the horror of the damage remained.

The feeling of the fresh air outside hitting my lungs should have helped, should have allowed me to breathe easier. It didn't. I could barely focus by the time we reached the engine and the pissed off, worried, confused words of my team weren't registering.

As the last of the flames died out and the hose was wound in, I leaned back against the engine, concentrating on pulling in air through the oxygen mask over my face. My final thought before the lack of air reaching my brain made everything go black...

I'd failed.

CHAPTER
Ten

I'd heard about it, read about it and seen it on the TV, but I'd never actually *felt* it.

That feeling when you're floating somewhere outside of the realm of consciousness, but you can hear and feel the world around you. I felt the warmth of a soft hand holding mine and heard the sounds of people bustling around.

But I wasn't there. Only in body, not in mind.

I could smell Carlie's perfume and feel her presence, I wanted to open my eyes but my limbs wouldn't respond. I mentally sighed, too exhausted and weak to care. What felt like ten minutes, but could have been ten hours later, I blinked into the harsh lights of the hospital ward and shook my head, or I attempted to. Everything ached. I remembered everything.

Every stupid thought and every reckless decision.

The elastic from my oxygen mask was irritating my face so I removed it and looked around. There were three other beds in the ward. One empty, two had elderly men in them, both were staring at me. Awkwardly, I shuffled out of the bed and walked on trembling legs to the edge of my section, pulling the curtain closed. I wouldn't be leaving any time soon and there was no way I wanted to share my space with anyone else.

Carlie shuffled in as I slid back into bed and she yelped when she saw me, "What were you doing up? Lie down, lie down," she fussed.

I scoffed, "Don't fret, Carlie. I'm fine."

"Fine? *You're fine?* You're not fine! You've been out for hours. Nearly an entire day actually. You have a collapsed lung, Blake! The doctor said they had to give you a...a..." she looked confused.

"A Bronchoscopy?" I prompted

"Yes, yes, a Bronchoscopy. Through one of those um..."

"Endotracheal tube?" I provided.

The woman had probably been checking her nails while the doctor was speaking to her but the way I felt, I didn't need her to fill in the details because I was trained for it. I knew the details, the processes and the recovery times.

And yes, I was already pissed off about it.

"Yes! That's the one. They had to sedate you, Blake! And the doctor said even a few seconds more could have been so much more serious. You could have died! You're not fine," she cried.

I fought the eye roll that threatened to escape. I was the one injured and she was the one fretting. I understood it, but I didn't agree with it.

"Babe, come here," I held out my arm and she climbed underneath. "I know, I'm not fine. But isn't that the point, it could have been worse, at least I'm alive."

"Yeah," she sighed. "You'll probably have to quit work though."

She threw out the statement like she hadn't just sliced me with a verbal blade. The agony of her words hurt more than any lung damage ever could.

She was right, if the lung didn't heal properly, the long-term effects could end my career completely. I wouldn't allow that to happen. Whatever the doctors told me to do, I'd damn well do it. Resting, sleeping upright, using an oxygen machine...hell, even if they told me to hang upside-down and bark like a dog. I'd be out of the hospital first thing and buying the damn collar. If it was going to help me recover quicker, I'd do it.

"I'm so glad you're ok. What happened though, Blake? The guys weren't here when I arrived but Ian was and he said he couldn't tell me anything."

"He couldn't tell you because he wasn't there. He's retired, remember. What do you want me to say, Carlie? It's a hazard of the job, you know that," I explained, leaving out the details.

The details.

I wheezed in a breath that had me coughing so hard, I thought my ribs were going to break. I screamed in agony, which caused another cough. A nurse came rushing into the ward, took one look at me in a state and forced the oxygen mask back over my mouth.

She stroked my back as she spoke, "Breath in," I did. "Breathe out," I did that too.

After a few seconds, the stabbing pains softened into an ache and the cough subsided. Admittedly, it was a little worse than I thought. I had never felt pain like it.

As my thoughts returned to the details of the fire, Zach filled my mind. Was he actually there? Was he hurt? Worse? I needed answers and I needed them that instant, "Carlie, where's my stuff?"

She frowned up at me, "Your stuff?"

"Yes, my clothes, my stuff from my locker, my

phone. I know Ian would have brought them with him if he came."

"Your phone. Your fucking phone? Christ, Blake, you just nearly coughed up your lungs, you still have an oxygen mask over your damn face and you look like shit but your only thought is where your damn phone is? What is wrong with you?" She cried in annoyance.

"Keep your voice down," I hissed. "You're exaggerating and overreacting *again*. Don't you think I should be letting people know that I'm ok?"

With a huff, she turned and lifted a sports bag off the floor, "Here. I'm going for a walk."

Well, at least with being injured, I managed a few minutes of normality. I sifted through the few texts I had from people asking if I was ok, replied that I was fine and lifted the phone to me ear.

"Midway Fire & Rescue," Harry answered.

"Harry..." I didn't get to speak further.

"Blake, holy shit! Blake! We've been waiting on an update," his voice drifted away from the phone and he shouted for the rest of the guys. "Are you good? Heard you had a collapsed lung. That sucks, man. Here, wait, I'm going to put you on speaker."

"What, you're too lazy to work now, thought you'd take some bed rest for a while, is that it Bossman?" Marc joked. "Seriously though, how are you feeling?"

"Are there any hot nurses on your ward?" Matt called and I laughed, then coughed.

Their silence was telling. My breathing didn't sound good at all.

"It's all good, lads. Four weeks rest and I'll be back to light activity," I guessed. "Listen, anyway, I rang because I wanted to get the facts from yesterday. Do we know what happened yet?"

My phone bleeped with an incoming call, but I didn't recognise the number so I sent it to answer phone and went back to the guys.

"Ha! Typical, Blake. Workaholic," they all shared a laugh before I prompted them for an answer. "Electrical fire, apparently. The place was an accident waiting to happen. I've been there myself before. Looked great at first glance, they've got the best equipment available and it's done up and shit. Safety wise though, it's bad. The fire escape was broken, the smoke detectors were always faulty and there were loose wires all over the place. Surprised this didn't happen sooner. I'm surprised the place ever passed its fire safety inspection."

"What about people? Everyone manage to get out ok? Many injured?" I asked, with my heart in my throat.

"No, actually. They were damn lucky. Couple of ladies got checked over but they were ok, just shook up I guess. The owner of the place turned up just as the ambulances did," he paused and I almost fainted. Zach was fine, not dead, not injured. I was the one laid up in the hospital for no fucking reason. "It was weird actually, the guy seems like a bit of a prick if you ask me. Jumped out of his car and started shouting his mouth off at everyone, but I get that, it's his business at the end of the day. But then he saw you go down, and I don't know..."

He trailed off.

"You don't know what? He saw me go down and what?"

"Well I don't know! Maybe he felt guilty or some shit, but he like, freaked the fuck out. He actually *punched* Dave in the shoulder when he tried to hold him back. He kicked out at the engine and called us all cunts. Told you, he was just a prick. Then he just vanished! Like, one second he's losing his mind about shit, we made sure you were safe in the ambulance, turned around and bam! The guy has disappeared. Personally, I told Dave to report him. We don't do this job to get attacked by idiots who can't handle their shit, but he reckons it was just heat of the moment and it isn't worth it."

I found it hard to believe the words he was saying, but he wouldn't make that up, he had no reason to. Realising I hadn't spoken, I hummed into the phone. It made no sense for Zach to react like that. It was *him* who was messing with *my* head, not the other way round. The urge to find a way to contact him roared to the surface of my mind.

"God knows. You're right, it was probably some misplaced sense of guilt or something. Anyway, I'm going to try let everyone know that I'm all good. Stay safe guys, see you sooner than you lot probably want me to!"

I hung up and stared at the phone.

The muscles around my ribs were starting to throb and I silently hoped the nurse would be back soon with something stronger than paracetamol to help with the pain. I flicked the phone over in my hand a few times, I needed to find a way to talk to Zach. It would drive me insane if I didn't get my answers, and quickly.

Remembering the call I received while I was already on the phone, I wasn't surprised to find the voicemail icon flashing, I pressed play.

"Blake, hi it's Zach. I just...I thought," the line went quiet for a minute, only the sounds of heavy breathing could be heard. "You know what, it doesn't matter. Hope you're ok."

The line went dead. Without hesitation, I pressed 'call back'. The phone rang and rang, then clicked off.

"Oh that's right, it's fine when you want to talk, but you can ignore me just as easily. Prick," I muttered, to no one.

"That's a bit harsh, don't you think? Although, I have been called worse," my head snapped up to the curtain, to where Zach stood, arms crossed over his chest. He had a bag dangling from his index finger and he looked...well, he looked *good.* "You look a lot better than you did yesterday. Is everything ok?"

Incapable of speech, which was becoming a very nasty habit any time that Zach was in the vicinity, I nodded. He stepped closer, closed the curtain behind him and threw the bag on the bed.

"I know flowers and grapes are what you're supposed to bring when someone is in hospital, but you don't strike me as the sort of person who would appreciate that. There's a few magazines in there, some junk food and whisky," he shrugged, looking almost shy. "I'm not sure you should be drinking if you're on meds, but honestly, the whisky was mainly for me anyway!"

He grabbed the bottle from the bag, untwisted the cap and took a long gulp. I couldn't tear my eyes away as his throat moved. Since when was swallowing, sexy?

No, I take that back, swallowing has always been sexy, just not in the same context.

"What's wrong with you?" I asked, noticing that his usual aura of confidence was missing.

He chuckled without humour, "What's wrong with *me*? You're the one who's breathing like an eighty-a-day smoker who just ran the London Marathon. Fuck,

Blake! You didn't see you! It was bad enough seeing my gym destroyed, but then you just...you just...*went down!* I thought you were dead."

It surprised me that he seemed so traumatised.

"I had a collapsed lung. I'll feel shit for a while and it hurts like a motherfucker, but I'll be fine. It's a hazard of the job. Sometimes things don't go according to plan and this is one of those times. I'm sorry about the gym."

"Fuck the gym!" He exploded. "It's shit thing that happened and it'll take forever to sort everything out but it's insured, so it's good. You could have died! I heard what those guys said, the ones you work with. You shouldn't have been in there by yourself and you took your mask off. Do you have death wish? I don't know *shit* about this stuff, but I do know you guys aren't supposed to take the mask off!"

"Zach..."

"No! No, I know, ok. You have to do your job and that's all good, it's an amazing job. But why? I think, I mean, you need to tell me why you took such a risk. It's stupid! You're not stupid, if you did that all the time, you wouldn't have been in the service for so long so I know it's not that," he started to pace the small space. "It doesn't make any sense, this shouldn't have happened..."

"I thought you were inside," I growled, interrupting his tirade. "What was I supposed to do, Zach? How could I have ever faced myself in the mirror again if I'd have let something happen to you? It wasn't like I made the decision to do it anyway, I just...I *had to*."

He stopped and spun to face me. Swallowing, his shoulders slumped and he rubbed the back of his neck.

"Fucking hell. Fucking hell, Blake. This is not good. I don't do this shit."

"What are you talking about? Don't do what shit?" I asked.

"This!" He flicked his hand out. "This, worrying about people. Bringing shit magazines and *snacks* into hospitals. Do you know that when they loaded you into that ambulance, I drove around for two fucking hours and I have no idea where I went. I don't remember! I just know I turned up, back at the smoking pile of rubble that used to be my livelihood and I'd lost two hours of my life. Have you ever been that worried? So completely driven insane with worry that you actually just lose hours of your life? Because I haven't, not before yesterday, and not before you."

I sighed, he wasn't really making any sense.

"So what exactly are you trying to say, Zach?"

"I think..." he stopped.

"Damn it! You think what?"

"I think I want you."

I frowned, "No offence, Zach, but that doesn't make any sense. You already made that obvious and," I lowered my voice to a whisper. "You had my dick in your mouth less than seventy two hours ago. Pretty certain I already knew that you wanted me. You're jittery and acting crazy because you want me? I don't buy it."

"You don't understand," he pressed, sounding panicked. "I don't do this. I fuck anyone as long as I find them attractive. *Anyone*. I never claimed to be a good person and I'd be a liar if I did. I don't even fucking remember the names of the majority of the people I've fucked and I...Don't...Care."

Rapidly growing impatient with Zach's nonsensical rambling, I reached out to grab his hand. His speech paused and his eyes fell to our joined fingers.

"Get to the point, Zach."

With a heavy sigh, he sat on the edge of the bed and moved our hands to his lap.

"You know I want to fuck you, obviously. But I'm like a spoilt child when it comes to sex and I'll have whoever I want, then go find the next person. That's not it though, what I mean is, I want *you*. We've spent less than three hours together, including right now, but my brain doesn't seem to care about that. I'm not sure even what I'm asking, but maybe, do you think we could...I want to *date* you or something. I want to *know* you."

Before I could respond, the curtain swept open and I snatched my hand away from his lap. The nurse, followed by Carlie. Her eyes flicked between Zach and I, then back again. I tensed, not knowing how much of Zach's words she had heard.

I was handed a tiny cup with tablets in and a glass of water so I swallowed them before anyone could speak.

"Um, hi Zach. What are you doing here?"

I watched him change in front of my eyes. His shoulders relaxed, he grinned and shrugged. His ego was showing again. The more I saw him, the more I was starting to think that was just a facade entirely. A mask that he put on each morning to face the world.

"When I found out that a fireman got hurt at the gym, I thought I'd come down and bring something to say thank you. It's a brave thing to do and who knows, maybe things could have been even worse and someone could have died if they hadn't been there. Seemed like the right thing do. Anyway, as you obviously know, I turned up and who's the hero of the hour?"

He lied so easily, even I believed him and I *knew* he wasn't being honest. It seemed as though Carlie did too when she cried, "Oh how lovely!"

She hugged him, then said to me, "See Blake, didn't I tell you that he was such a good guy?"

"Yeah, Carlie, you were right. He *is* a good guy."

I put extra emphasis on my words so that he could start paying attention. Sleeping around doesn't necessarily make you a bad person.

"I'm going to shoot off anyway. It was good to see you, and I hope you feel better soon," as he stood up to leave, Carlie reached for the bag of gifts that he had bought with him and he snatched it away. "No! Um...sorry. I'll just put these away before I leave."

He shoved the whole bag in the little cupboard next the bed and flicked two fingers in a wave as he left.

"Well that was odd," Carlie mused.

It actually was odd, so I agreed with her.

"Anyway! I was just talking to the nice doctor outside and he said he'll be round to talk to you after dinner, which is about fifteen minutes, but that he'll be recommending that you stay here for four or five days so they can monitor you and keep an eye out for signs of infection or further respira...breathing issues. You'll be right as rain in no time, he said! I'm going to head home before the dinner rush and evening visiting hours," she shuddered. "You know how I feel about the germs in these places, especially when there's so many people around. I'll pop by tomorrow though, after I've found a new decent gym."

She leaned down and kissed me on the cheek,

lingering for a few seconds, "I'm glad you're ok, babe. Love you."

She strolled away and I was left staring at the closed curtain in shock. I know, I know, I definitely couldn't be putting myself forward for husband of the year award, but I was willing to try. I was still making mistakes and I had a lot to make up for but I would never have left Carlie alone in the hospital less than an hour after she woke up from a life-threatening injury. Who does that?

There was still some fight in me but I was beginning to wonder if that was a waste of both our time. Didn't I deserve to be happy too?

With the new painkillers flowing through my system, I gave up on trying to work out my life and closed my eyes.

CHAPTER
Eleven

The first rays of sunshine were touching the horizon when I woke up, telling me that it was still far too early. My stomach rumbled, reminding me that I hadn't eaten, so I reached for the buzzer to call a nurse.

"What's wrong?" Zach's sleep-filled voice sounded from the side of me and I jumped.

"Fucking hell, you scared the shit out of me," I hissed. "What are you doing here?"

Rubbing his eyes awake, he sat up further up in the chair and leaned forward.

"I couldn't sleep last night. I was just pacing the apartment, not knowing what to do with myself. So I came back. Must have fallen asleep at some point, but damn this chair is *not* comfortable."

He stretched out his back and extended his bent legs.

"Why do you need a nurse anyway?" He asked.

I looked at the buzzer in my hand, trying to remember why I had needed it, "Oh, I didn't really. I just need something to eat."

He scoffed, "Trust me, there aren't nearly enough nurses in this place to help you with that. I'm sure it won't be long until the breakfast comes round. Why don't you just have something from that stuff I bought you for now?"

"Oh yeah, I forgot I even had that," I reached for the bag but paused when Zach laughed quietly. "What?"

"You didn't open it yet."

"No, I fell asleep not long after you left. Why?"

He shrugged with a grin, "Just take a look."

Curious as to why he found himself so funny, I opened the bag and emptied it all out onto the bed.

Magazines, crisps, chocolate & a few pieces of fruit. Nothing funny.

"Thank you?" I said, though it sounded like a question.

Still grinning, he leant over and pushed one of the magazines forward. A fully-nude man winked up at me from the cover and one of the articles said 'Which position is right for you? Are you getting enough from your man?'. Once it hit me exactly what sort of magazine he'd bought, I scrambled to hide it under the pillow and scowled at him.

"Are you crazy? Why would you do that? I don't want that," I fumed.

He didn't even have the grace to look guilty, "Well, at first I thought it would be funny. Then I started to wonder if it might actually help you figure some things out."

I closed my eyes and my teeth clenched. There was a lot of things I needed to figure out at that point but looking at the front of that magazine made me want to throw up. I didn't find men attractive and seeing one naked had no effect on me whatsoever. His obvious attempt at humour just fell flat and I could hardly bring myself to look at him.

"You might be ok with all this, Zach, but I'm not.

I'm a married fucking man for crying out loud. What if Carlie had have found that?"

"It would be difficult for her to find it considering she's not here, is she? She fled this place seconds after I left and she didn't even hesitate. I was still sitting in my car wondering if I should be leaving at all and she comes strolling out like she doesn't have a care in the world. She jumped in that shiny, girly car and just took off! Face it, Zach, that woman cares about no one but herself."

"She doesn't like hospitals."

"Who does? No one *wants* to spend time in a place that's full of death and disease. Don't make lame excuses for her."

Things were starting to get heated. What the fuck did he know about the way a wife should behave? He'd admitted it himself, that he was the world's biggest slut. The thought fled as soon as it came because in a way, he was right and I'd thought the same thing myself. I just didn't want to admit it.

"Look, this is getting us nowhere. Just...just don't buy me things like that ok, I hate it."

He shrugged, "It was just a joke, Blake. I think you're overreacting, but fine, it won't happen again."

He fell silent, but kept his eyes on my face. He was looking at me like I was a puzzle he needed to solve. Part of me wished that I could just give him the answers, except that I didn't even have them myself. I'd overreacted and he'd called me out on it.

"I'm sorry, I didn't mean to bite your head off."

He scoffed, "I'm not a woman, Blake, and I'm also not stupid. You can react however you want to react because they're *your* emotions. I'm a big boy, I can take it. I don't want or need your apologies. I should have known that you wouldn't see the funny side just yet. Don't worry about it, yeah?"

I narrowed my eyes slightly. It seemed far too easy, too simple, for that to be the end of it. I was too preoccupied with waiting for him to storm out that I almost missed it when he asked me a question.

"When's your birthday?"

"What? Why?"

"Just answer the question!"

I told him, "March fifteenth. You?"

"June thirtieth. So you've just turned, what? Thirty? Thirty-one?"

"Thirty-five."

His eyes bulged, "Seriously? Damn."

"What? What's wrong with being thirty-five?" I asked, confused. It wasn't exactly old!

"Well, you just don't look a day over thirty. Blake, does it bother you that I'm only twenty seven?"

I knew he was younger than me. Did it bother me? No.

I huffed out a breath, "Zach, you're a *guy*. Do you honestly think that the fact you're a few years younger than me is going to bother me, when the fact that you have a cock doesn't?"

"Well, when you put it that way..." he paused. "No, I guess not. Favourite colour?"

"Green. Are we really doing this?"

"Playing twenty questions? Yep," he confirmed with a nod. "I told you. I like you and I want to know more of you. If that means I have to revert to being a seventeen year old boy who doesn't know how to hold a proper conversation, then that's what I'm going to do."

I opened my mouth to laugh, when my breath escaped in a rush and sharp pains shot through my lungs. I wheezed, coughed and tried patting my chest to relieve the pressure but I couldn't seem to suck in a breath. Through the pain, I focused on Zach's worried face and tilted my head towards the oxygen tank, "Mask. I need the mask."

He jumped up, grabbed the mask and placed it over my face. The coughing subsided moments later and my lungs filled with air. There is nothing, *nothing*, worse than the feeling of not being able to get air into your lungs. It's almost like you are watching yourself suffocate.

"And you wondered why I couldn't stay at home," Zach joked shakily.

"I'm fine, don't worry. This will pass. I could do with some more of those painkillers though. My ribs are aching like a bitch."

He ran to the door of the ward and returned seconds later with the little cup, the painkillers and a cheeky grin.

"That was quick," I noted.

His grin morphed into a smirk, "How do you think I was able to stay at your bedside all night? That petite little blonde nurse is a sucker for a wink and a smile. Most of them are."

"You're unbelievable," I shook my head while he agreed.

"I'm going to have to go and deal will all the boring insurance crap for the gym, but I'll be back as soon as I can. There's nothing more horrible than being on your own when you feel like shit. Do you need me to bring you anything back?"

I should have said no and that he shouldn't bother coming back, but like he said, there is nothing more horrible than being on your own when you feel like shit.

And if nothing else, I just wanted the company.

"Honestly, yeah. Is there any chance you can bring me some actual clothes? I'm not staying in this thing," I lifted the neck of the hospital gown. "For the next however long."

"No problem. Phone charger?"

"Oh! Yeah, an IPhone charger," I added.

"Gotcha. I'll sort it. If you think of anything else, you can call me and I'll get that too."

"And Zach," I called before he left, he turned back. "Thank you."

He spun back towards me and climbed onto the bed, causing my lips to part in shock. Putting one hand on the pillow next to my head and the other on my neck, he leaned down, his breath whispered across my lips.

"You're welcome, Blake," his lips brushed mine. "Just so you know, this is what you do when you actually give a damn."

Then he plunged his tongue into my mouth and took control. His fingers snaked into my hair and held my head still while he kissed me. My body reacted on instinct and my cock hardened. All too soon, he pulled away. Noticing that I was struggling to catch my breath, he handed me the mask again and laughed lightly.

He gave my cock a gentle squeeze, "Let's hope this'll keep for a while because there will be no more kissing for you until you can actually breathe."

Thirty-five. I replayed my age over and over in my head in attempt to fight off the urge to sulk like a four year old who had been told they couldn't have any more candies. Zach saw straight through me and smiled.

"There's plenty more where that came from, but I'm going to need you to get better for me first, ok?"

"Yeah, ok," I agreed.

"See you soon."

I threw my head back and groaned. I had no self-control where that man was concerned. None. Zero. I was beginning to understand that maybe things were the same for him, though I would never understand why.

CHAPTER
Twelve

"You're pissing me off," I growled, rapidly losing patience.

"I'm not pissing you off, you're just pissed off," Carlie stomped her foot like a three year old throwing a tantrum. "One more night, Blake, That's all. Just one!"

"I'm only going to say this once more and if you don't listen, I'll just do it anyway. I am not staying in this god forsaken fucking place for another night. I'm not even staying for another hour. I've tried asking you nicely, that didn't work, so either fucking help me get all this shit together, or leave."

Carlie huffed and crossed her arms, "You're behaving like a child! What's one more night when you've been here for six already? This is the best place for you to be when you're still not well, Blake."

Instead of repeating everything we'd been going over for the past twenty minutes, I just moved around her and started putting all my belongings on the bed. I had been in the hospital for six, very long, very boring days. I needed out. I wasn't one hundred percent healthy, far from it, but I was ready to go home. There was no difference between resting and taking a few pills in the hospital or at home. I was leaving.

I hadn't needed the oxygen mask in two days and the pain was starting to subside...slightly. I was under no illusion that being at home would help me recover any quicker, but I did know that I wouldn't have to stare at the same patterned curtain for hours on end each day and that was enough for me. I could *not* sit around for one more second without going insane. Carlie, however, was convinced that I needed to be a good little boy and do as the doctor said. Well fuck that. Enough was enough.

"We'll I'm not helping you. If you want to put yourself at risk of infection and ignore what's best for you, I want no part of it."

I sighed, "I just don't care anymore, Carlie. I told you, help me out or leave. I'm done talking about this. I'm not a child and I don't have to listen to you whine on about this. The decision is already made. Why do you care anyway? It's not like you've been here playing the doting wife the last week, have you? Huh?"

"I *knew* you were pissed about that!" She screeched. "I told you, I had overtime at work!"

"You didn't have overtime twenty-four hours a day, Carlie. I've seen you twice! *Twice!* In six days! And one of those visits, you stayed for ten minutes before you faked a yawn, said you were too tired and left. Even the guys from the station have been here more often than you. Your excuses are bullshit and so is your constant whining. Just go, I'll find my own way home."

She stared at me, not moving an inch, but I was done. I wasn't going to keep arguing, I just didn't have the energy. Then she sneered.

"You're their boss, it's called kissing ass, Blake,

and they're all experts at it. It's not like you needed me here anyway. Your new best buddy hasn't been very far away from this place all week, has he? Good old Zach has been playing the nice card a little too often as far as I'm concerned."

"Jesus Christ, Carlie. You can be such a bitch sometimes. They *care*. It's not about ass kissing. And Zach? The guy has lost everything. His whole life revolved around that gym and right now, he just needs a friend," I ignored her muttered 'you would know' comment. "I was hurt at *his* property, he feels guilty. Why shouldn't he come here? He wants the company and considering my wife couldn't give a fuck, so do I."

I was so, *so* done with the fucking conversation. She was being a bitch, that much was definitely true, but she was also hitting a little too close to home with her words. Zach had kept to his word, he'd been back. Every single day, he'd come by. Sometimes he stayed, sometimes he was just popping by. I didn't care either way, as long as I saw him.

Yes, my fascination started with something new, something different. Turns out, I actually really liked him. Still, things were far too complicated for me to be looking too deeply into anything.

"Lovers tiff?" Speak of the devil...

Carlie threw her arms up in frustration, "Oh look! Your knight in rusty armour is here. Well he can deal with your grouchy ass because I'm out. Good luck, Zach."

"I'll just see you at home, Carlie," I told her.

"Don't bother. I don't want to see you."

And with her parting shot, yet again, I was left staring at the flick of her hair as she stormed out. It was official, my life had gone crazy. My wife, the caring, funny, beautiful woman I'd married, was long gone. I did *not* like the woman who had replaced her.

"Trouble in paradise?"

I sighed, "Just don't, Zach, ok? I'm tired, I'm in a bad mood and I just want to go home," I glanced at the door that Carlie had just left through. "Or maybe not, as the case may be."

He followed my line of sight and I must have realised that I just wasn't in the mood because he nodded.

"Come on, I brought another sports bag to fit all this stuff in. We'll get you all packed up and then I'll go find a doctor to get you discharged."

My lip twitched, I didn't even have to ask and he knew, "You're too good to me."

"Oh I know, I know. You can make it up to me by sucking my cock later."

My face snapped up to his to see if he was serious. He hadn't even come within a foot of the hospital bed since the last time he kissed me.

"Are you serious?" I queried quietly, glancing around the ward to make sure no one was listening.

"Do I look serious?" He raised his eyebrows but I shrugged. You never could tell with him. "Yeah Blake, I'm serious. Blue balls doesn't even come close. It's been more than two weeks since I've stuck my cock in anything wet and warm. Let's face it, you owe me."

I laughed in shock, "You're unbelievable!"

"Yeah you've said that before, but you have no idea how unbelievable I can really be. Come on, you don't need to stay here any longer than necessary."

"That was cheesy, even for you," I complained, but started packing my things away with his help.

Within the hour, I had a month's worth of

prescription painkillers, a lecture about discharging myself early and a disapproving look from my consultant but I was finally leaving. I sat in the passenger seat of Zach's car wondering if Carlie would have actually calmed down by the time I got home. Twenty minutes into the drive home, Zach flicked the left indicator and pulled into the driveway of a modest little two-story house.

"Wha..." he cut me off.

"Look, do you really want to go home? Knowing that Carlie doesn't want you there right now and no matter what you say, that pain in your ribs is worse than you're letting on. Anyone with half a brain can see that, just by the way you're carrying yourself. This is my house, I figured we'd stop here, you can rest, chill out for a while and give Carlie a call in a bit after she's had time to cool off."

"Yeah," I nodded. "Yeah I think I'll do that."

"Good, because a taxi from here to your house would cost a bomb!" He joked. Asshole.

Leaving my two bags in the car, I heaved myself out of the seat and followed Zach into the house. It was...empty. Even for a guy. I mean, there was a sofa, a TV, an XBox and nothing else. Same with the kitchen. Cooker, microwave, fridge. Nothing personal at all. Even a show home would have had more life in it.

It was plainly decorated. Browns, beiges and creams. Wooden floors, black furniture and not a hint of personality. I halted my train of thought when I realised that I genuinely didn't give a fuck about wallpaper or furniture.

The dining room was where I broke my silence and had to say something.

"Why is your dining room a home gym, when you

own an actual gym?" I asked.

He laughed, "Picked up on that did you? This is *my* space, Blake. Work is work and as much as I love it, it's not where I relax."

"It's a nice place, Zach, but this whole house is *your* space and the rest of it looks like no one lives here. Where's all your stuff?"

"That's where you're wrong. This isn't my space, it's hers," he opened the backdoor and I heard an excited yelp before a beast came bounding towards me. I tensed waiting for the impact but the second Zach told her to stop, she did. She sat at my feet, her tail wagged and her tongue lolled to one side. "Blake, meet Daisy."

I awkwardly crouched down, ignoring the protest from my ribs and gave Daisy a scratch behind the ear, "Hey girl!"

"You have a Cocker Spaniel called Daisy?"

"Yep, and don't be fooled. She's had the best training money can buy and in front of you, she's the perfect dog. The minute you turn your back though, she's the devil in dog form. Hence the fact that this house is empty. If she didn't eat it, pee on it or scratch it to death, I've hidden it."

I laughed. It felt so *normal*.

"You want a beer?"

"Can't. Painkillers, remember?"

"Shit, yeah sorry," he cringed.

"Zach?" I called and waited for him to look back at me. "Why are you nervous to have me here?"

"You want the honest answer?"

"No, I want you to lie to me," I deadpanned. Stupid question.

Releasing a heavy sigh, he began, "Because in that hospital, it was just talk. I could talk to you and get to know who you really are. I saw you at your weakest and you didn't care, do you know how rare that is?" He didn't wait for me to answer.

"Here, this is my world. This is my reality. Fact remains, I'm out of my league with this. In an hour, maybe two, you'll be going home to your wife and we both know you're eventually going to phase me out. I'll be a distant dirty secret and you'll go on as if nothing happened. You'll sort everything out, maybe have a kid or two and grow old, *with Carlie*. I knew from day one that I shouldn't get attached, but then *you* came to *me* the third time and I thought, maybe there's a chance. I've done nothing but think about it this week though, Blake, and I just can't be that guy. Thing is, I'd let you have us both and actually be happy with what I could get. Then it'll be what? A week? A month? Maybe more. But I'll always know, somewhere in the back of my mind, that you go home to your wife at night. Meeting you, it's just made me realise that I deserve something real and I'm not giving that to myself by fucking anyone I lay my eyes on."

"I don't know what you want me to say, Zach," I said, because I really didn't.

His words had floored me. *He* was the one who pushed *me*. *He* was the one who wrapped his mouth around *my* cock. *He* was the one who came to see *me* every day in the hospital. Yet, *he* was the one who was telling *me* that enough was enough. Fuck that.

"Actually, I do know what to say," I stood up and brushed myself off. "Fuck you, Zach."

He went to speak but I stepped right into his face, our chests were touching so I put my palms to his pecs and pushed. He stumbled back.

"Fuck...you...You're the one who came into *my* life. I didn't ask for it and I didn't ask for *you*. How dare you assume that I'm the one who gets to have everything here? You can't force your way into my head and then say 'sorry, too complicated up in here so I'm leaving'. It doesn't work like that. You think I want to be torn in two because I'm married to a woman I love, yet I can't stop thinking about a man who makes my head spin? I fucking don't. You made that happen. It's all just a game to you, isn't it, Zach? Some personal challenge to fuck with people's minds. Speak to Carlie, she's the master of sexual coercion, maybe you can share tips. The pair of you would be a force to be reckoned with." I was breathing heavily by the time I'd finished but I had one last card to play.

I dropped to my knees and dragged Zach's trousers down.

"Whoa, what are you doing?"

I fisted the base of his cock and only had a moment of hesitation, of fear, before I said, "Paying off my debts," and took him in my mouth.

It started as a game, as a final 'fuck you', like somehow he'd be the one who suffered if I gave him a taste of what he'd given me. It would never have worked but the shock of feeling him swell on my tongue made my blood heat. I pulled back, sucked lightly on the tip and then lowered my head. His moans of pleasure spurred me on, I wanted to prove that I wasn't the person playing mind games...by playing games with his body instead.

Pre-cum leaked on to my tongue as I licked the underside of his cock and swallowed his length. I groaned as his taste filled my mouth and pulled his hips closer, taking him as deep as I could. I gagged and he tried to pull back but I forced myself to relax and took him deeper still. He locked his knees to stay upright and that's when it hit me. Being on my knees for him wasn't about giving him control or power over me. I held all the control right in the palm of my hand.

Or in my mouth, as the case may be.

The thought made my dick weep. I couldn't give this up even if I wanted to. Although, I just wasn't sure that I actually even wanted to anymore.

I replaced his cock in my mouth with my own fingers, soaking them in moisture, "What were your words to me, Zach? Just relax, let me own all of this..."

I reached in between his legs, fondled his balls, then moved further and slid my fingers between the cheeks of his ass. The heat radiating from his tight ring made me shiver in anticipation. Instinct made me push one finger inside his body, and lust made me add the second. Zach grabbed hold of the weight rack to hold himself up and bit out a muted, "Fuck!"

My fingers pulsed in and out of his ass, my mouth worked his cock and his hips pistoned forward as I sucked harder.

"Fuck, fuck! Please..."

I buried my fingers deep, determined to make him lose control. The first streams of cum shot to my throat and my breathing faltered. I wouldn't fail him though. I scissored my fingers, stroking his inner muscles as they tensed and contracted and he moaned my name as he filled my mouth with his seed.

CHAPTER
Thirteen

I. Was. Lost.

Reckless decisions. Wayward thoughts. Uncontrollable lust. There were any number of reasons that my mind had taken me to a place that I couldn't come back from but none of them seemed to be enough.

I pushed up from the floor, looked around in desperation and headed towards the stairs in search of bathroom. It was becoming a nasty habit of mine, but the need to escape was too powerful. I turned the lock behind me and rested my hands on either side of the bathroom sink. Staring at myself in the mirror, I didn't recognise the man staring back at me. Since when was a blow-job, a punishment?

My face looked the same, but at the same time, couldn't have been more different. My jaw still prominent, my nose still slightly curved and my hair still longer on the top than the sides. But the change was in my eyes. The green of my irises looked deeper, like you could fall in and be trapped there forever.

The answers to all the questions swirling in my brain was hidden in those eyes. They were my own, but even I couldn't get inside.

I smacked the sides of my head with the heels of

my palms.

I felt like I'd fucked up a lot in my life, but nothing as monumental as this. Somehow, I'd figured it wasn't quite as bad if Zach was the one making the first move, but the second, the third? That was all me. At any time I could have, and should have, told him to back off. Told him he was wasting his time because I was a happily married man.

And therein lay the issue.

Because I *wasn't* a happily married man.

I was fucking miserable.

My wife didn't really like me, no matter what she claimed. I spent more time at work than at home. I was learning new things about myself that I wasn't sure I liked, and more than anything, I was falling in love with a man faster than I could think to stop it.

I swung the bathroom door open, bound and determined to storm out of Zach's front door and never look back but when I stepped forward and straight into the man himself, all my good intentions fled.

"Are you going to leave?" He asked nervously.

I hated the timid way he spoke. Despised it. He wasn't fucking timid or nervous. He was supposed to the one who had his head together, the one who could tell me exactly what I was doing.

I shook my head, not meeting his eyes, "I don't know, Zach. I should leave..." I trailed off, not entirely sure what I wanted to say.

"I know," he whispered. "This is a whole new level of fucked up, Blake. You know that right?"

"Of course I fucking know that," I spat.

"Look," he sighed. "I refuse to do this. Look at the state of you, you're a mess and I'm half the problem. You're not happy. Just...just go home and talk to

Carlie. I know what I think you should do but..."

"It's so easy for you isn't it? So simple. I've known you three weeks, Zach! Three goddamn weeks and you've turned my world on its head. Now, what? You think I should go home and tell my wife to fuck off because I've decided I want to try cock for a bit?"

"I never said you should leave her for me, Blake, so don't put words in my mouth. I'm just trying to help. In *your* life, she makes you unhappy. Ask yourself why are you really sticking it out?"

Driving my hands into my hair, I growled, "I don't fucking know, ok? Is that what you want to hear? That I don't know why we bother staying together."

"Stop thinking about what I want to hear! Think about what *you* want."

"I need time. I need you to give me time," I decided.

"Then that's what you'll get. Come on, I'll take you home."

"No," I put my hand on his forearm. "I'm going to phone a taxi. I need time, and when better to start than right now?"

He tilted his head and narrowed his eyes, "Alright, go."

It was said softly, but I still caught the hint of disappointment in his tone. I ignored it because if I didn't, I'd never leave his house at all and it was something that I had to. I heard Zach calling a taxi and I ran to his car and retrieved my bags.

"I never meant for this to happen you know?" He said whilst I waited for the taxi. We were standing on the front porch because I couldn't allow myself to go back inside. "It wasn't like I planned this. Don't get me wrong, that first night, it was never about Carlie. She used to be a nice enough woman, always self-centred but still sweet. And she's beautiful, insanely so, but it wasn't about her. It was always about you."

I clenched my jaw, "You're a lot of things, Zach, don't add 'liar' to the list of them. You'd never met me before that night."

"True. That doesn't mean it wasn't about you. *All* about you. Do you actually know how long I've known Carlie?" He asked and I shook my head, I had no idea. "Two years, Blake. Pro-Weight's has been mine since two weeks before my twenty-fifth birthday and she was a member already when I took over. Oh she couldn't wait to talk, like it was some insatiable need she had. My husband this, my husband that, look at this picture of him, or this one of us together. But it was never about how special you were. It was about how special *she* was because she had you. I don't have secrets, as ironic as that is now. At the time, I think my openness made her feel threatened in a way, like she had a point to prove. When she started banging on about how lonely she was, how little attention she was getting, I found my way in. Call me sly, hell, call me worse, I don't care. She offered the threesome and I accepted. *For you,* and for me. When you opened that front door, all pissed and angry because you thought I was after your wife, something I'd be thinking for a while, was confirmed...your taxi's here."

Damn that man for always managing to crawl his way that little bit further into my mind. I believed every word he said because the words were so raw, you can't fake that sort of thing.

"Time, Zach. Just give me time, yeah?"

"Yeah," he sighed.

I jumped into the taxi, wound down the window and shouted, "Zach, wait!"

He turned back from the door and I asked, "What was it that you'd been thinking?"

His smile was somehow sad, but his eyes shone.

"That I've been in love with *you*, since the day I met *your wife.*"

The taxi pulled away from the curb and I sat back in the seat.

"Stop!" I shouted, scrambling forward.

"Give a minute, just, give me one minute and I'll be back yeah?" I chucked the taxi driver a few quid to hang around and sprinted from the vehicle. My lungs burned from the few feet I ran, but I pushed through it. I hammered my fist on the front door and he swung it open.

I pulled him by the front of his t-shirt and crashed my mouth to his. He matched my force with his own desperation and clawed at my hair with his fingers. I sucked on his tongue, begging to keep his taste in my mouth for just a little longer, then pushed away. We were both breathing hard and my chest was rising and falling rapidly with the effort.

"Just time," I said.

"Yeah, Blake. Just time," he nodded.

Then I turned and jogged back to the taxi.

It was the longest drive home of my entire life.

CHAPTER
Fourteen

Time.

It's such an underestimated concept.

We never think about how the same amount of time can mean so much or so little.

You're waiting in line at the bank, five minutes feels like five hours. You're rushing to get that last job of the day done, five minutes feels like five seconds. Isn't that odd?

It's all about perception.

In annoyance or frustration, in longing or patience, you perceive time to be longer than it actually is. The exact opposite applied for me.

I just wanted a little time.

I had three months. Or ninety-eight days to be precise.

Life went on, nothing changed. I was stuck in a loveless marriage with a wife who I genuinely thought hated me. I was starting to think she lived to make my life miserable, like I was being punished. I took that punishment because I deserved it. I woke up every day feeling like the fraud that I was. I was acting at life. The new master of deception.

I went to work, I went home. Then I woke up the next day and did it all over again.

An endless cycle of misery and self-loathing.

It was pathetic.

"For fuck sake," I growled in annoyance.

I had been staring at the station rota for half an hour and not making a single note. Every day was the same and my lack of concentration was quickly becoming an issue. Ian appeared in the doorway and I shook my head, "Didn't you retire?"

My attempt at humour fled when he stepped inside my office and shut the door behind him.

"What's going on?" I asked.

Crossing his arms over his chest, he looked over the rim of his glasses at me, "I think you need to take some time off, Blake."

I frowned, "I've only been back for five weeks. Why would I take time off?"

"I don't know what's going on with you lately, but you're not the Blake that we all know and care about. You're lazy, distracted, and sometimes downright ignorant and you're going to lose the respect of those men out there."

Ouch. That hurt.

"I'm fine, Ian. Yes, my head hasn't been in the game lately but it's all good. I'll sort it. Thanks for the warning."

"You don't understand, Blake. I'm not asking you, I'm telling you. Take some time off. Two weeks, a month, just don't come back until you're ready to be part of a team again."

My anger spiked but I breathed in and held it, to calm myself down.

"No offense, Ian, you know I respect you but that's just not your choice to make," I returned, shocked at his thoughts.

"That's the way you want to do it? Fine. In that case, first thing tomorrow, I'll be reporting all the failures from this station to the county manager and giving him my recommendation that the station manager should be replaced with immediate effect."

I shot up from my chair, "You can't do that! The county manager is your damn brother, he'll fire me on the spot."

"Why would he fire you if 'everything is all good' and 'you'll sort everything'? Legally, if you're not doing anything wrong, the worst he can do is keep an extra keen eye on things here," he said.

"Fine," I spat. "I'll take some time off, but fuck you for doing this to me. I don't need this shit."

His voice softened, "This is for your own good and you'll thank me when you get back. What happens when a member of the team gets distracted, Blake?"

It's a quote that we were all taught in the first week of basic training, it's then drilled into you every day until graduation.

I sneered at him, "People die," he nodded, but his face fell into a scowl when I finished. "Except that I'm not part of a team now, am I? I sit behind a desk, point fingers and write reports. So no, no one dies, no one gets injured...the worst that's going to happen from me being *distracted* is that I'll get a fucking papercut. You can shove your patronising shit where the sun doesn't shine. How long are you going to be able to keep coming back here, Ian? You're too old and you're no better for this place than I am, or anyone else for that matter, yet you still think you're the best thing that ever happened to that team out there. Well, newsflash old man, they're *my* guys. You win this round, but don't think you'll be sitting in that seat for long because that's my job, my office, and *my team.*"

I slammed the door behind me and stalked across

the concrete floor towards the exit. I could feel the guys' eyes on me but I was too enraged to talk to them. What gave Ian the right to come barging in making threats whenever he felt like it?

Fuck him. Fuck his cocky brother too. I knew that bastard would find a way to fire me if Ian told him to.

I slumped into the driver's seat in my car and slammed my foot on the accelerator. Life just wanted to fuck me over in every way. The punishments just kept coming.

I made the journey home in half the time it usually took, only to find Carlie and her dad, both dragging suitcases over the front lawn. I jumped from the car and Roy scowled at me. I was *so done* with the whole day.

"What's going on?" I asked.

Carlie gave a 'look' to her dad, who shook his head and took both suitcases to his car.

"I'm leaving, Blake."

"Why now?"

Why that day? Why that time? I knew she would leave eventually, and as awful as it sounds, I wanted her to. I wanted to rid myself of the guilt that was weighed on my mind for every second, of every day. But really, how much could one man take in the space of an hour?

She hiccupped, and a tear slipped from her eye, "We're just not us anymore. I'm not leaving *you* though, I'm just leaving here. I think, if I go and stay with my dad for a bit, maybe we can work on being us again. I don't know? We'll date, we'll go right back to the start and try again. Anything is better than this honey and you have to admit that."

"I know, Carlie. Do you even think it's worth trying? Or is this just it, and we're done?"

"Don't you think I'm worth it?" She returned, her voice rising and a scowl shadowing her pretty features.

And there it was. The real Carlie.

The whole 'leaving' wasn't about her finding the right way to fix our marriage, it was about making a statement. I'm leaving so that you'll realise how much you miss me and you start doing anything you can to get me back. Even her tears weren't real. I stared back at her for a second, just wondering if I could find *anything* that I was still in love with; I came up blank.

When did I let this get so bad?

I should have left months ago. Possibly years.

"Honestly? I really don't know anymore. You're always angry and I'm always miserable. People don't just wake up one day and change how they think. I don't know if we've just grown into different people. I'll try Carlie, but I make no promises."

Her palm connected with my cheek and pain splintered across my face. Maybe honesty isn't always the best policy.

"Fuck you, Blake Thomas. Damn right you'll try, because I'm not giving up on this marriage. I refuse to be a divorcee."

"Just go to your dad's, Carlie, but listen," I paused to make sure I had her full attention. "Don't ever fucking hit me again, got it? You're alarmingly close to losing whatever shred of class you're still holding on to. I love my wife. I do, and I wouldn't lie about that. Problem is that I haven't fucking seen her in years. Honestly, Carlie, go to your dad's, wallow in your own self-pity about your failed marriage and make sure everyone in the gossip tree knows what an awful husband I am. While you're at it, make sure you take the time to think about *you.* It takes more than one person to break up a marriage and I think, when you delve a little deeper, look a little closer to home, you might find out a thing or two about yourself. Remember though, darling, You threw the blade, you just need to keep praying that it's not you who lands on it."

"Was that a threat?" She asked. Clueless.

"Jesus Christ!" I threw my hands up. "Were you always this stupid? I genuinely don't know how we ever held a conversation. Just go."

I slammed the front door and collapsed back against it, sliding down to the floor. I buried my face in my hands and roared.

Time.

What a fucking joke.

CHAPTER
Fifteen

The lake stood still in the silence.

Peace, tranquillity...space.

I felt like I had died and gone to heaven.

Week two of my solitary confinement at the cabin and I was finally starting to make some decisions. I had formed the beginning of my plan of action.

It had taken all of five minutes after Carlie had left, for me to receive the phone call that gave me some semblance of life back. Harry had called from the station phone, telling me that he was on my side and so was the rest of the team. It was a nice gesture and one that he didn't have to go out of his way to do. I told him that I was going to take some time anyway, that I had some stuff going on at home and I wanted to get away for a while. I think it shocked him that I'd told him, although I left out the details, of course. He pretty much told me that they'd always have my back but that I should do whatever I needed to.

Then he told me about his cabin.

Out in the middle of nowhere, a two-room cabin by a lake and I would be completely alone.

I had the keys in my hand and my foot on the accelerator within half an hour and I hadn't been home since. I wasn't ready to face reality yet. I'd turned my phone off the day I arrived and left it in the car.

I fished, I drank, I stared out across the lake...and I thought about *everything*.

The calmness of the water always fascinated me. Hundreds, if not thousands of creatures were living their lives under the surface and yet, as far as the eye could see, it was all utterly still. Eerily so.

It became my metaphor for the time I was there. How the trauma of someone's life, will have absolutely no effect on anyone else's. Did I have the right to speak to Ian the way I had, or Carlie? Of course not. I would have to deal with the consequences of that as soon as I got home and that was half the reason I was putting it off.

It's hard to swallow your pride in any normal situation. Apologising to two people when I completely meant the words I'd said was going to be a tough pill to swallow but it was time to start putting my life back together. That was why I stood staring out at the lake for one last time before I left. The car was packed up, the cabin was locked and the engine was running.

Yet I hadn't stepped away from the lake.

It seemed so important, so relevant, I couldn't let go.

Just like everything else in my life apparently.

With a heavy sigh, I turned and slid into the car. The magazine that Zach had jokingly brought me lay open on the front seat. Surprising myself, I'd actually looked through it, I even read parts of it...and hated it. The thought of touching another man in *any* of those ways made me cringe. The thought of doing them with Zach? That was a whole other story.

The journey home felt like I was voluntarily walking into shark infested waters and the serenity I had gained from being away was peeling away with every mile. Step one was well underway.

I drove the long way around when I arrived back in town and smiled for the first time in months when I saw that Zach's gym was finally rebuilt and open again. I was happy for him, but I didn't stop.

I drove straight home.

Spending the next few hours putting everything away and giving the house a quick clean, I actually felt better than I had in years. This was *my life*, damn it! I moved to bedroom, ready to empty my bags, and I froze in the doorway. The bed had been slept in. Carlie's pyjamas lay in a pile at the foot of the bed and the wardrobe door was open.

She'd been there.

And if the state of the room was anything to go by, she was back *living* there.

The front door flew open and she screamed my name. I couldn't move.

Her footsteps bounded up the stairs and she threw herself into my arms, "You're home!"

"What's going on?" I rasped, dreading her answer.

"Oh! It took me all of a single night of staying at my dad's to realise that you're right, babe. I'm so sorry that I left. That's not going to work. If we're going to make us better, I need to be here *with* you. I've missed you, did you have a nice trip?"

Fuck. Me.

I shook my head, "It doesn't work like that, Carlie. You left because we're not working any more. It was the right thing to do."

She smiled, huge.

"I'm so glad that you understand. Now we can work on making each other happy again!"

"No."

Her head snapped back, "What? Of course we can."

"You can take the bed, I'll sleep on the sofa until I can sort something else out. We're finished, Carlie."

I said it and I meant it. There was no going back. What I had done meant that I didn't deserve her anymore. More than that, it made me realise that I could never make this work. I just didn't want to. I walked out the house, leaving her staring at my back in feigned shock.

Somehow, I managed to remember the way back to Zach's house and parked outside. His car was on the driveway and I frowned, I didn't actually think he'd be home. I didn't particularly *want* him to be. I needed an extra few minutes to compose myself. The shock of seeing Carlie so soon after getting home had blown my plans to shit.

After sitting outside for longer than could be considered normal, I sucked in a breath and walked to the door, bringing my fist up to knock twice. Zach's shadow moved behind the frosted glass but the door didn't open. I could see that he'd stilled.

"Let me in, Zach," I called.

His shadow jerked and the door handle shook. His face appeared first, then his shoulders and finally, when he opened the door all the way, I felt like I could breathe.

"Hi."

His eyebrows rose, "Hi."

"Can I come in," I asked and he moved backwards to let me by.

I purposely brush my hand across his hips as I

moved and hid my smile at his sharp intake of breath. His standoff-ish manner wouldn't last long.

"You're late."

My forehead creased, "What?"

"Almost four months, Blake. You've been gone for *nearly four months,"* he spat. "Why are you here now?"

I didn't suspect it would be easy, I'd stopped all contact with him for a long time. The anger in his voice though, was masking his disappointment and that killed me. I had been so blind.

"I know, I'm sorry. It was just what I needed to do. There's no more though, Zach, I want you, if you still want to..." I broke off in doubt.

I didn't know if he'd met someone else, or changed his mind. Frankly, as selfish as it was, I had only been thinking about how I was feeling.

Zach's body crashed into mine and his tongue plunged into my mouth. The kiss was desperate and needy, full of anger and intensity. I grabbed his hips and pulled him between my legs, feeling his length harden against mine. I had *craved* that feeling. I groaned into his mouth, shifting my hips to gain the friction I knew we both needed.

"I missed you," he moaned as I dug my hands into his ass cheeks. His lips slid down my neck and the rough stubble covering his face spread goose bumps in its wake. He paused, "Your lungs? Your ribs?"

I shook my head, "All good. Healed within a couple of months and I only get the odd pain or wheeze now."

"I missed your voice," he kissed my collar bone. "I missed your smell," my chin. "I missed the way you move," my shoulder. "I missed this..."

His hand snaked inside my trousers and squeezed the head of my cock lightly, "Let me try something?"

Catching his eyes, I held them when I swore, "I'll let you try anything."

He knew I meant it too. He grabbed the back of my neck with his free hand and pulled my head forward for another breath-stealing kiss. My knees weakened.

"Watch," he growled as he shuffled his own trousers over his hips and his cock sprung free. I licked my lips, I knew how he tasted and I wanted more. "Later, Blake. Right now, just *watch* and feel."

He pushed his shaft against mine and I cursed at the first contact. Something so subtle shouldn't be able to feel so fucking amazing. Grabbing both of us in his hand, he slid his fingers down to the root and back up, twisting his hand at the head. The combination of his soft foreskin, opposite the roughness of his palm caused sweat to bead at my temples. I hadn't had an orgasm since the last time I saw him, not even by my own hand. I knew I wouldn't last long.

He took my hand in his and guided it downwards, linking our fingers together. Following his lead, I grasped our aching cocks in my palm and allowed him to guide my movements.

"Come with me," he gasped, burying his face in my neck.

My dick throbbed at his words, leaking pre-cum into my hand. The added lubrication forced me to thrust forward and I bit out a curse when I felt the first hot spurts of Zach's come hit the head of my cock. My balls tightened, my toes curled and I growled out his name as he bit down on my shoulder, draining himself of his orgasm.

I held out, wanting to watch him before I lost control but seeing his body react had lust igniting in my veins. The heat of my orgasm climbed from my toes, my calves, my thighs and I shuddered, grabbing hold of Zach's forearm to hold myself up and I followed him over the edge.

I sucked in a shaky breath and confessed, "I didn't come here for this."

Zach huffed out a laugh but didn't reply. His face was still hidden in my neck and he still had one hand keeping hold of my softening dick. His other drifted lightly from my hip to my nipple and back, soothing my racing heart.

"I'm glad you're here," he admitted.

The corners of my lips kicked up, "Me too. With Carlie acting insane at home, it feels good to be here with you."

I failed to notice his body turning to stone. I failed to notice the way his head snapped up. I failed to notice the flash of pain and disgust that crossed his face. I did not, however, fail to keep talking.

"The woman is driving me round the bend. I took some time away, went and spent two weeks out at a cabin by a lake and thought I finally had it all figured out. Within two hours of being home and she shot that all to shit. I just...I needed to see you."

"Get out," he snapped, pushing me away from him, but my legs refused to work. I was frozen in shock. It didn't make any sense for him to have changed his mind in a matter of seconds.

"Just leave, Blake. I don't want you here anymore. You fucked up, huge, and I'll never forgive you. It's pretty fucking clear right now that you're poison to everyone who loves who. I can't and won't, ever forget that. Leave. Don't ever come back here and don't ever, *ever*, contact me again. Understood?"

"What? I...no," I stuttered.

"Fuck you. Fuck you for not realising that I'm worth more than this shit. You can't come here, expecting me to be your side fuck while you *still* have a wife at home!"

"Wait, what?"

I replayed the previous conversation in my head.

"Carlie left, Zach. She knew it was over. I went away for a fortnight, I literally just got back a few hours ago and she was just...there! Acting all crazy and saying how we were going to be together again. I told her no! I'm not *with her*, my marriage is over and, well, that's it really."

He shook his head, eyes to the floor, "It really doesn't matter. I haven't heard from you in *four months*, Blake. I wrongly assumed that you were taking that time to pull yourself together. The guy standing in front of me right now, he's exactly the same. You said it yourself. *She* left *you*. What does that say, Blake? I'll tell you. It says you spent the entire first three months, twelve whole damn weeks, doing nothing. You didn't tell her you were leaving, you didn't repair your relationship with her, you didn't phone me and tell me to never contact you again. You just did nothing! It took Carlie to make that first move and *that* tells me all I need to know. I won't be anyone's consolation prize."

No, no, no, that wasn't how it was supposed to go.

He wasn't supposed to be so mad at me.

Daisy barked, scratching at the back door, begging to come in. He moved to let her inside but I was frozen to the spot.

I *had* to make him see that he was first for me

now.

First, and only.

CHAPTER
Sixteen

"I'll be filing for divorce. I'm not staying with her, I'm not sleeping with her. Fuck it, I've probably said no more than a hundred words to her in months!" I explained, when he returned to the hallway.

"Then you need to leave! Or she needs to leave!"

"You don't get to make that decision for me," I spat, losing patience with the whole conversation. I mean, I'd been home less than a day and I already wanted to say 'fuck it all' and go away again. When did people become so difficult? Realistically, I knew he was right, but throwing it in my face all the time didn't help the confusion swirling in my brain. One way or another, I was fucking someone over. I already knew, deep in my gut, that I would be going home and packing my things for good. Thinking about Carlie's reaction though, sent my stomach twisting in panic.

"You're a coward, Blake. That's the truth of it and if you thought anything of me *at all*, you would have made sure she was long gone before you came back to me. I *know* things have been tough for you, but for crying out loud...*man up!* Cut ties and be done with it. It's not like she's going to stick around for long once she realises that you're gay."

Without thought, my back shot straight and I barked, "I'm *not* fucking gay."

I blinked in shock. Then blinked again.

One of Zach's eyebrows rose and I tried my best to ignore how fucking sexy that tiny movement was. Every - single - thing the man did, messed with my head.

"You're not? Then what are you? Because I'm pretty sure I have a cock, and I'm even surer that you were jacking it not ten minutes ago."

"That's...it's...I," I stuttered. He stayed silent and I managed to pull myself together, at least on the outside. "It's just...you."

His face softened and I winced.

Way to reveal everything, Blake.

"Isn't that the point, Blake? You can't keep us both, you know that. It's not fair of you to *expect* that. What we're doing right now is wrong, we both feel it every time we're together, so you need to make a decision and stick to it. Can you give up on a marriage of ten years, to a woman you still love? Or you can you go back to her fully, knowing that if you do, I'll let you go. I'm not going to fight your decision if you need to give up on us. Three months was hard because I was waiting for you. Knowing you're never coming back would be a different story, I'd deal with it. I know your guilt is killing you right now, but don't be thinking that it isn't just as bad for me. Carlie was my friend. Yet, I'm stabbing her in the back every time she comes to the gym and I plaster a fake smile on my face to mask the fact that I'm jealous as fuck that *she's* the one who gets to share your bed every night. I hate that I feel like that and the guilt, it burns inside me," the pain in his voice made me blanch. "But I put up with it, for you, for us. That can't go on forever though, it's too much and we'll be causing more pain for everyone in the long run. So Blake, the choice is yours."

"Why are you doing this, Zach? Why now? You already know I want you."

He looked incredulous and shook his head, "Why am I doing this? Fucking hell, sometimes you can be so stupid. I *waited* for you. Four months, Blake and my loyalty never faltered once. Yet you leave for all that time, come back to me with a smile and promises of trying this with me, when your fucking wife is still waiting at home for you! I really thought you were just struggling to deal with everything but it isn't that. You really are just behaving like a kid throwing his dummy out the pram. You said you needed time and I gave it to you. Instead of using that time to get your head together, you ran away and came full circle. Now we're right back where we were at the beginning. I deserve more than that, as much as I don't like her behaviour lately, so does Carlie."

"You think I don't know that?" I asked, genuinely. "*I didn't ask her to come back, Zach!* I came home and came *to you*. I don't want her, I want you and I'm changing my whole life for you, everything about me."

He interrupted, "And there's your problem. I'm not asking you to change anything about yourself for me. You think that you wanting to be with me is about change because I'm a man. It's not. You don't just wake up one day and decide you're gay, Blake. It's always been there and yeah, maybe I gave you the permission you needed to explore it but isn't an illness and I didn't cause it."

He was wrong. So, so wrong and I told him so.

He shook his head like he didn't believe me, so I explained.

"Remember that magazine you bought me as a joke?" He nodded, so I continued. "Do you know that I actually read it? I have *never* been attracted to a man, Zach. Never even looked twice. The things I read, the pictures I looked at and - *I shuddered* - the videos I watched online. They made me sick to my stomach. It was the most disgusting thing I've ever experienced. Do you think I think of you that way? Or that I ever could? I wasn't hiding a part of myself for thirty-five years. That part of me just didn't exist. Maybe I am gay and maybe I'm not, but it's not the label that bothers me because I don't care what people think. I felt like I needed to work out why I have such a powerful reaction to you but then I realised that it just doesn't matter. If my attraction to you is that powerful, I can ignore the fact that you're the same sex as me, it's never going to go away, Zach. I don't have any decisions to make. I'm already with you. This delay isn't about keeping you both, it's about doing damage control to make sure that Carlie doesn't get hurt more than she obviously will. I've done some bad things recently but I'm not a bad person and I'm just trying to protect her."

He nodded slowly, "Ok. I'm sorry. You have to admit that it looks bad, Blake. You say all the right things but actions speak louder than words and you're not moving anywhere."

He had a point.

"I'll prove it to you then."

"When?" He questioned.

When? That was a good question. I wanted to say I would prove it right then. That I'd go home, tell Carlie we were done, grab my things and leave. But that was both unrealistic, and slightly cruel on Carlie's behalf. The thought made my heart squeeze and thump heavily in my chest. I might not be in love with her anymore, but I would never hate her. You don't throw away ten years without pain, that much I knew, but I just wanted to minimise it.

"A week," I decided. "Give me a week."

"One week, Blake. I'm too far gone to keep hanging on to something that isn't mine. I was fine without you for twenty-seven years, and I'll be fine again. I'm not some lost puppy that's going to follow you around. One week."

As much as I despised the thought of him being just fine without me, I understood. He wasn't lying either, the force behind his words and the determination written all over his face said he'd give up on us if I didn't fix things within a week.

A week.

Right, because it always came down to time.

I kissed him and left, not wanting to hang around anymore with the tension growing. We were only keeping a loose hold on that line between fucking and fighting and I wasn't willing to push it.

The following day at home, I paced the lounge. I'd managed to avoid her the day before but that plan wasn't going to last long. Carlie was in the shower and when she called my name, I went. Shouting through the bathroom door, I asked what she needed but my jaw dropped when the door swung open and she stood naked in front of me. Hand on hip, she tilted her head, "I forgot my towel, could you go and grab it for me please?"

She smiled.

Speechless, I nodded in silence and moved away.

Even when we were happy, she didn't do things

like that. I knew it was a game. Her way of proving that I still wanted her. Honestly, I did. She was beautiful and she worked damn hard to keep her body so perfect. But I'd learnt the difference between want and need already. Wanting to have sex with someone is just a drop in the ocean compared the how it feels when your body is consumed with need.

So her naked body caused no reaction. Anything I felt for her disappeared a long time ago.

"Here," I handed her the towel but she made no move to cover herself.

Dragging her teeth along her bottom lip, she blinked in false innocence.

"Do you um, want to join me?"

Fuck.

Shit, fuck and damn. She left me with no choice.

"No," I sighed. "No, Carlie I don't. Finish your shower, we need to talk."

Her lower lip trembled but her eyes were dry and she slowly dragged the towel upwards to cover her skin. I didn't hang around to talk any further, I jogged down the stairs and threw myself down on the sofa. I was dreading what had to happen. When I heard the shower shut off, I sat up and braced my elbows on my knees.

She came down in her gym gear, with a clean towel draped over her arm.

"Where are you going?" I asked, already knowing the answer.

"Gym."

"No, Carlie, wait. We need to talk," I reminded her.

She waved her hand in the air as though it wasn't important, "We can talk later."

"No, we'll talk now."

"Listen, Blake. I have things to do, whatever it is can wait. I won't be too long just two or three hours," I interrupted her.

"You walk out that door right now and it really doesn't matter how long you're gone because I won't be here when you get back."

"Oh? Are you going out?"

As much as she was pretending to be clueless, no one could be that stupid. She wanted me to spell it out? I'd do it.

"No, I'm leaving. For good."

She laughed, "You forget, honey. I tried that. It doesn't work."

"Carlie, you *pretended* that you were leaving me, to try and make me beg you to stay. You were playing mind games and you lost. We've been over for a long time, it just took me a while to realise it. Why are you being *this* person?"

The ditzy facade finally fell.

"Why? Why, Blake? Let me see. Could it be because I don't want you to leave? I don't want to give up on us. I don't want to be divorced. I don't want to have to learn how to live life *on my own*. Some lonely spinster with ten cats! I don't even like cats!"

"Have you heard yourself? It's all about image with you! You don't want me to leave because you're worried that it will make *you* look bad. People will pity you. Well you're just going to have to get the fuck over it. I've put up with this shit for long enough now. We're making each other miserable and it's not fair on either one of us. Do you honestly think that being on your own for a while is worse than spend the rest of your life with a man you don't love? Hell Carlie, you don't even *like* me!"

"I like you! I love you!" She cried, losing her grip on control.

"No, darling. You love the *thought* of me. You love the thought of all your friends and family looking in from the outside and seeing the picture of perfection. Oh look how lucky Carlie is to have the perfect home, the perfect husband, the perfect life. You can't stand the thought of anyone knowing that we failed. That *you* failed, because you don't give a fuck about me and I'm not sure you ever did," I never raised my voice but that didn't mean my words didn't cut through the room like a sharp blade.

"It's not true! You're twisting everything. You just want to leave because, because...well I don't know why! But I'm not giving up that easily. You think we're over but we're not."

Apparently, my words weren't working. Then Zach's speech flashed through my mind and I said, "Fine. Words don't mean anything to you. Maybe actions will. I don't love you any more, Carlie and I will *not* be coming back," I grabbed the bag of clothes I'd thrown together and headed for the door.

"You can't leave!" She screamed. "You can't because...I - I - I, I'm pregnant!"

I tripped over my feet and stumbled forward, swinging around to face her. She looked as shocked as I did.

"You're pregnant?" I whispered in horror.

Her face had drained of all colour and she swallowed heavily, looking anywhere but at me.

"Err, y-yes."

The stutter was her tell. She was literally standing in front of me, lying through her teeth. My forehead wrinkled as I stared at her, trying to figure her out. I could never, and would never, understand why women thought lying about things like that would fix anything.

"Jesus Christ," I croaked. "Jesus fucking Christ, you've lost your mind. Are you really so desperate that you have to make up babies to keep me here? Newsflash, Carlie, I wouldn't stay even if you *were* pregnant."

"You want kids, Blake. With things with your dad, you wouldn't leave me with a baby on my own, you'd want to be involved." She stated, not knowing whether that was the truth or not.

I shrugged, "Doesn't matter either way considering you're lying through your teeth and you are *not* good at it. You're right, I'd never leave any kid of mine to grow up without a dad, and you misunderstand me. What I'm saying is, even if you did have my baby growing in your belly, I wouldn't stay *with you*. But fuck you for throwing my dad in my face. We're done."

I shut the front door quietly as I left. The thought of staying for a single second longer made me want to throw something.

CHAPTER
Seventeen

I drove around for a few hours looking for a decent hotel.

The weather seemed to matching my mood as the rain fell in sheets across the windshield. The radio was off, the sound of the window wipers played on repeat in the silence. I was officially driving away from my marriage with a bag full of clothes and a few extra bits.

And I felt free.

The black cloud that had been hanging over my head for so long was just...gone. Maybe that was why it was raining so hard. I snorted at my own thoughts. I was free, but it wasn't over. *That* was why I'd had a permanent scowl on my face since I'd left my house.

I swerved to avoid a pothole and slammed my foot on the brake as the car came within millimetres of mounting the pavement.

"Fuck," I breathed. I needed to find a place to stay for the night, and quickly.

Problem was, the one place I wanted to be, I wasn't sure I would be welcomed with open arms. Instead of driving straight to Zach's house, I swung by the gym first. Not seeing his car in the car park, I went in anyway. The rain hit my face and I cursed my choice of clothing. By the time I made it to the reception, my white t-shirt was soaked to my skin and my jeans were hanging off my hips with the weight of the water dragging them down. I held the side of the waistband in my fist and approached the desk, my shoes squeaking on the tiled floor with each step.

The same receptionist greeted me, "Good afternoon!"

I just looked at her, surely it didn't *look* like I was having a good fucking afternoon.

"Zach here?" I asked.

She pursed her lips but said she would find out.

"Sorry, he hasn't been in all day. He might be later though," she advised.

Nothing was going to plan. Then again, nothing ever did.

"Can you call him, please?"

"Oh, we're not allowed to call his personal phone."

I leaned forward, placing both hands on the desk, "Listen. I'm a friend. He knows me. You can clearly see that I'm in a bit of a situation, I'll be sure to pass on the message about how helpful his wonderful receptionist was if you could ...please ...just call him."

Mirroring my movements, she stood for her chair and leaned forward. Her hands were rested on her hips when she semi-repeated, "Staff members are not allowed to call Mr Black's personal phone unless in case of emergency. As you can see, everything here is running perfectly fine. No emergency. You're more than welcome to take a seat and wait for him on the off chance he turns up."

I grumbled under my breath. Yes, she was doing her job. Yes, I could actually despise her for it.

"Fine," I replied, then reached forward and took the phone off her desk. She gasped in outrage. I dialled Zach's number and waited until he answered.

"Maria, everything ok?"

"It's Blake."

He didn't miss a beat, "What are you doing there? And how come you're using the office phone?"

"Can you get here? I'd rather not have 'little miss helpful' here listening to this conversation," he said he'd be right there but before he hung up, I called his name. "I don't suppose you keep a spare set of clothes here do you?"

"Um, yes. I'm not even going to bother asking why. Just go into my office and you'll find whatever you need. The code for the door is 'C' five, seven, nine, five, then press the hash button."

"Got it. And Zach, thank you." I placed the receiver down and handed the phone back to Maria.

"Thank you, you're a sweetheart," I lied, with a smile.

I repeated the door code over and over in my head until I reached the door to Zach's office, and was greeted with brick wall. The place where his office used to be had been renovated after the fire and everything looked completely different. Clenching my teeth, I stormed back to reception.

"He moved his office after the fire, didn't he?"

Maria smiled smugly, "Yes, sir. He did. Would you like me to direct you?"

Rubbing my forehead with my palm I gave her an equally fake smile, "If you could, that would be great."

"Easiest way is, straight on until you reach the

lifts, take the lift to the second floor, follow the edge of the room until you reach the treadmills and Mr Black's office is second on the left after the security cameras."

"Thank you."

Following her directions was easy. I punched in the code and entered the office and my eyebrows rose. It was huge. Probably designed to match his ego. Shutting the door behind me, I grabbed a clean t-shirt off the rail, threw it on the back of the chair and stripped out of my wet clothes. I peeled my boxers down my legs and added them to pile. I turned to reach for the t-shirt, panicked and dived behind the computer chair when the lock bleeped and the door swung open.

Zach laughed, quickly shutting the door behind him, "Don't usually get that view when I walk into my office.

I stood up, not caring in the slightest that I was naked and I mock-scowled at him.

"A knock would have been nice."

He didn't respond, he stared at my body. His eyes flitting from my chest, my thighs, my stomach, my cock. He licked his lips and I groaned, "Jesus. Don't look at me like that."

His grin was wicked.

"Why is it that we've been playing around this thing for a while, and the only time I've ever seen you naked is that first time?" He asked.

I shrugged, "Usually because you get your hands or mouth on my cock and it's all over before it really starts."

He looked curious.

"That's true," he paused. "Don't get dressed on my account! Two things though. One, why are you here? And two, why are you naked? Not that I'm complaining, of course."

"I'm naked because the heavens came down on me as soon as I got out the car and it took me far too long to work up the courage to come in here. Stupid move, I know. I'm here right now, because I didn't want to wait a week. You were right and I just needed to cut ties. I grabbed a bag full of my shit and left. Not until Carlie decided that she was going to ask me, when she was naked, if I wanted to shower with her. That was enough for me and I left. I just...I didn't have anywhere to go and you were the first person I thought of," I explained honestly.

Fighting a smile, he bit the side of his mouth.

"So it's done?"

"It's over," I confirmed.

"You're still naked," He pointed out, needlessly.

"Mm hmm," standing taller, I crossed my arms over my chest and watched Zach's eyes fire as they fell, once again, to my erect dick. "What are you going to do with it?"

"I've had the taste of you on my tongue for months, I've had the feel of you in my hands and the essence of you on my skin. No more playing, Blake."

He shrugged out of his t-shirt, whipped off his joggers and kicked his trainers to one side.

"I want you to fuck me."

I swallowed. His words sounded like the challenge that they were. A challenge I was more than willing to accept.

"Get over here," I rasped, voice thick with lust. In three strides, he was in front of me, breathing my air. His cock stood long, thick and hard. The thought of me fucking him obviously had a major effect on his libido because the tip was already beading with pre-cum. I bent at the waist and licked it clean. His head flew back when I lightly ran my tongue along the underside and then sucked.

I stood up, pulled his face to mine and plunged my tongue into his mouth for a quick, passionate kiss, "I've never loved anything as much as I love the taste of you in my mouth."

Gently biting my shoulder, he whispered his agreement. Voices filtered through the door and I froze.

"Don't worry," he whispered. "They can't come in here."

"They could hear us though," I noted.

"I don't care. I can read your thoughts though and I'm thinking that you're just going to have to fuck me quietly. Got it?"

I nodded, my nerves suddenly kicking in. I walked in a circle around him. The long lines of his body, the planes of his abs, the way the muscles in arms raised and flex every time I touched him. I committed it all to memory. I slid my hand up between his shoulder blades and pushed forward.

"Bend over the desk, brace your hands on the edge and whatever you do, don't let go, ok?"

He did as I asked, the motion causing his ass to spread and my eyes lasered in. I sunk to my knees behind him and let my instincts take over. I wanted to touch him *everywhere*. Starting at his ankles, I dragged my hands upwards, over his calves and the backs of his thighs. I squeezed his ass roughly.

"You're perfect, Zach. Fucking perfect, everywhere."

The gravelly tone of my voice made him moan and he let his head fall to the desk.

"Fuck, Blake. You've got to do something. Touch

me, jack me, fuck me *and fill me*. I don't care. Any of it, all of it. I need it. I swear I..." He broke off on another long moan as I rubbed the stubble on my face against the cheek of his ass and extended my tongue. I licked a path from his balls to his hole and circled. I licked and sucked at his skin, revelling in the sounds escaping from his throat. Unable to stay away any more, I leaned over him, his ass cheeks cradled my cock and I had the slightest hint of just how fucking amazing it would feel to be inside him.

"I need a condom, Zach."

He groaned in annoyance, and I silently agreed. No more waiting. Blindly feeling around in the top desk drawer, he sighed, reached around and shoved a line of condoms and a little sachet of lube into my palm. I slid the condom over my cock, but hesitated with the lube. I'd never used it. Never had to.

Did it go on him? Or on me?

I emptied it onto my hand and shared it with the other. Reaching down, I grabbed my aching cock in my fist and stroked myself, coating the condom with the lube. At the same time, I teased Zach's entrance with the tips of two fingers, smoothing the liquid around the puckered hole and slipping one finger inside. So fucking tight.

"Tell me I'm not going to hurt you," I demanded, failing to disguise the need in my tone.

"You're not going to hurt me, Blake. Stop teasing me and *fuck me!*"

I lined up the head of my cock at his entrance and paused.

"Do it, Blake. Right fucking now, I want you inside me, I want..."

I pushed slowly through the tight ring of muscle and heat consumed me. His ass squeezed my cock like a vice, the muscles sucked me deeper.

"Fucking hell," I grunted, at the same time Zach moaned, "Holy fucking shit."

"Never," I panted as my hips curved forward, slowly sinking into his ass over and over. "Never, ever has anything felt so fucking perfect."

And I wasn't lying.

"Faster, Blake. Harder."

I pushed faster, he started pushing back. He met my thrusts with equal need. I gripped his shoulders, pulled my cock back so that just the tip was inside his body, and punched my hips forward.

"Fuck!" Zach screamed.

I stilled thinking it was too much, but he reached back and slapped my thigh, "Don't fucking stop, I'm so close."

"Your ass is squeezing me so tight. Fist your cock, Zach. Jack it. Do it fast and do it hard because I can't hold on for much longer."

He fisted his cock and violently jacked it from root to head and back. My rhythm faltered and my balls ached. The sight of him laid out for me, desperately jacking his cock, was too much. I sunk my dick to the root, buried in his ass and spilled my cum into the condom. As the final drops emptied, I pulled out. Zach was still fisting his cock, reaching for his orgasm. I pushed two fingers into his ass and stroked his inner bundle of nerves. His legs shook, his knuckles turned white on the desk. I twisted around, dropped to the floor and slid underneath him, keeping my fingers deep. His dick leaked across my chin, I relaxed my jaw and took him into my mouth. He thrust forward, the head of his shaft touching the back of my mouth and the thick, warm jets of his cum ran down my throat.

Holy shit.
I wasn't sure that either of us would ever recover.

CHAPTER
Eighteen

"This feels weird," I admitted, not tearing my eyes from the TV. Stroking my fingers through Daisy's fur.

Hours later, we were at Zach's house after he had asked me to stay. It was where I wanted to be, but I still wasn't sure that it was the right thing to do. It felt like I was taking advantage, in a way, but he insisted and honestly, I just wanted one day without any arguments. So I was staying.

But it felt weird. Too normal. Too average.

I could feel Zach's eyes on me, "What feels weird?"

"This," I tilted my bottle of beer towards the TV. "Us. Absolutely nothing about us so far has been normal. Just sitting here, drinking and watching the TV, it feels weird. I'm sort of waiting for the next drama to happen."

"It was an intense situation, Blake. I'm not saying life will just be all daisies and buttercups now, but we're allowed to have a night in front of the TV without the world caving in around us," he joked.

"I think I'm falling in love with you," I blurted, then froze. I hadn't meant to say that. I don't what I was planning to say but it wasn't that. I felt it, sure, but there was no ready I was ready for him to know that. "Forget it, it's too soon. It doesn't matter."

"Calm yourself. You already know I love you, it's good to know it isn't one-sided, but it's also not a surprise."

Wow, that was a little cocky, if not completely arrogant. I told him as much. He laughed but shook his head.

"It's not cocky, you misunderstand me. Have you not wondered why you have no issue talking about sucking cock, you can fuck me like a pro, you'll get down on your knees and swallow my dick to the back of your throat...but you can't even fathom the thought of touching another man?"

As he spoke, my mouth filled with saliva. I longed to do everything to him that he'd just said. But he was right, when I thought about having another man bent over and taking my cock, I could practically feel my skin turn green with nausea. I nodded and pursed my lips, "It's all I ever think about," I agreed. "It makes no sense."

"It makes perfect sense."

"Why?" I asked, genuinely curious.

"Because, Blake, we're soulmates."

I scoffed, then paused, and scoffed again. Soulmates. What a ridiculous thing to say. I wasn't one of those who believed in such things. I believed you just liked spending time with someone, so you worked at making a relationship and keeping it. Fate, destiny, all those other 'higher powers', just didn't make sense to me.

"You can scoff all you like, but I'm right. Think about it, would you have ever considered leaving Carlie and uprooting your entire life, for anyone else?"

No, I wouldn't have but that was just about timing. Had Zach come along at any other time in our marriage, there was no way I'd have done any of it. He just would have been another face in another day. Nothing more and nothing less.

"Ok, let's say this. How long did it take you to decide that you thought Carlie might actually be *the one*?"

I shook my head, I couldn't remember, "Three months? Six months? I don't know. I asked her to marry me when we'd been together for a year and a half. We were married six months later."

"Blake," Zach began. "Do you realise that we've only known each other for about four weeks? Yes, in terms of time, it's been five months, but we didn't see or speak to each other for almost four of those. People don't fall in love in the space of a few weeks. Deny it all you want, you were in love with me by the second week. Call it fate, insta-love, or whatever else people call it these days but whether you believe it or not, it happened and it stayed. I love you because you have the other half of my soul, Blake and that's not something that happens every day."

"You really believe that?"

He tilted his head to the side, "Which bit?"

"All of it. But mainly that I have the other half of your soul."

"I don't just believe it, I know it. I feel it right down in my stomach, in my bones and in my cock. It's so easy to throw out words like 'own', but that's how it feels. Like you own me. And I hope, now, or one day soon, that I'll own just a little bit of you too."

I felt that. The ownership thing. Where you just feel like your entire body doesn't belong to you, or like someone else's name is etched into the surface.

Was that what soulmates were about? Still seemed like a bit of a stretch to me and it must have shown on my face.

"Don't think logically because feelings don't follow the rules of logic. That about how it *feels*, Blake. Picture this. A new member joins my gym, he's tall, dark, and his body is sculptured the way most men can only dream of. He comes to me for help, tells me that he's not quite sure how to safely move up to the next set of weights. He's lying, clearly. The way he's built, he knows how to do the perfect workout. He just wants to be close to me, to touch me," I could feel my blood pressure start to rise. "He's a charmer, he knows exactly what to say and when to say it. Innocent touches here, small compliments there. I'm oblivious, I don't notice he's doing it because why would I? I'm with you. Then he steps it up, his touches become more often, his words are suggestive. He makes it clear that he wants me and he's going to do everything in his power to have me."

"Stop!" I yelled, my pulse roaring in my ears.

The volume of my voice made Daisy bark and her head jerked up. I shushed her and stroked her behind the ears. She calmed down instantly

I could picture it all. Every last word was burned into my brain and it hit me that he was right. It wasn't about jealousy, because I didn't feel jealous. I felt white hot anger searing through my limbs and paralysing my body. The man was a figment of imagination and yet I felt the uncontrollable urge to hunt him down and commit grievous bodily harm.

Ridiculous. So fucking ridiculous. Yet, it was there and it made me understand exactly what he was trying to tell me. He had his claim on me because he was getting my cock, true. But it was more than that.

He'd claimed my soul and I'd claimed his.

That bond was unbreakable.

Maybe soulmates really did exist.

"You've had enough. It doesn't feel good, does it?" He noted and I shook my head. No, it really didn't feel good.

"How do you know this stuff?"

He shrugged, "Before you? I didn't. But I pay attention, Blake. I watch and I listen. I'm also not too afraid to admit exactly how I feel and I think that made things transparent for me. I told you. I fell in love with you before I'd even met you. I'd seen pictures, I knew everything there was to know about you from someone else's perspective, but I'd never met you. Never talked to you or felt you, never listened to you or learnt your smell. But there's no denying that I was in love with you. You can't tell me that doesn't mean something, because it does. I don't make a habit of going after married men, Blake. Difference is, you were *mine*. Carlie didn't deserve you and she still doesn't, but if you weren't mine, I would never have let myself get involved. Too complicated, to dramatic, it wouldn't have been worth the effort or the aggravation."

"Why does that make me feel like I have a shit ton of pressure on me, right now?"

He smirked, "Because you still need to catch up."

I agreed. I knew I loved him, I knew I wanted to be with him, but the rest of it, I hadn't yet admitted to myself and I wasn't sure how to.

Sighing, I rested my head on the back of the sofa.

"I'm going to have to tell my mum, she's going to want to meet you and I'm going to have be transported back to the eighties."

At the swift change in topic, his head jerked up

and his brow furrowed.

"Why the eighties?"

"Because Zach, there's a reason that I try not to see my mum all that often. She's crazy. Not in an 'I'm going to become a mass murderer' sort of way. She's harmless. She's just nosy, and flighty, and she thinks she's still twenty-five. She's stuck in the eighties, meaning any time I spend with her, I'm stuck there too. Don't be surprised if, when you meet her, she has the photo albums out within five minutes, looking at naked baby photos of me and she's offering to show you her *impressive* belly dancing routines."

He barked out a laugh, "You're joking."

"I wish I was. You'll see for yourself soon enough."

The air felt thick and I stared at him, the realisation that we were really going to do this, finally sinking in and hitting home. His head moved up and down slowly, "Yeah. Yeah, I guess I will see for myself."

He offered me another drink and I shook my head. Our conversations seemed to be deep and weighty, I didn't want to add more alcohol to mix and say something that I couldn't take back.

"What about you? Close with your parents?" I asked.

His lips twitched, "My dad, surprisingly, yes. Mum died when I was younger but my dad is amazing. He's the reason I have the gym."

"How so?" I enquired, interested to learn something about him that didn't include sex.

"He fronted me the money, simple. I always knew what I wanted and I'd worked hard to save, but a building that size and the equipment to go in it doesn't come cheap. The bank may as well have slammed the door in my face for all the help they were when I only had a measly deposit for a mortgage. He sold his holiday home in Mallorca, sold his car and pretty much put down his life savings for me. I was approved for the mortgage, and had some leftover to make the place look good. Don't get me wrong, he'd worked all his life and I didn't want to take the money but he called it an 'early inheritance', refused to take the money back and then took off in his campervan for faraway lands and only comes back every now and then. He calls often though, last week he said something about Italy and cheese. I switch off most the time because that man can talk more than I can."

He was smiling as he spoke, the love for his dad clear on his face. I realised that it was the first time I'd ever seen him truly relaxed and it was the way I wanted him to stay. We talked for a few more hours about family and life. I skimmed over the facts when he mentioned work because honestly, I didn't even know what was happening myself. I knew I needed to go back eventually though. My savings would only last for so long and considering I needed to find somewhere to live, I needed to keep the small amount that I had.

We talked, we laughed and we learned.

I got my dick sucked, returned the favour and spent the night sleeping next to my soulmate.

It was probably the most memorable day of my life.

CHAPTER
Nineteen

"Well, well, lads. Look who's decided to come crawling back to us!" Matt joked, the second I hit the station forecourt.

I smiled and flipped him off. I hadn't realised until my feet reached the front doors, exactly how much I missed the place. Or how much I'd missed the guys. It had taken all of fifteen minutes after my shower that morning, to realise that I didn't want to put things off anymore. Getting my life together, meant facing everything head on. I wasn't, however, looking forward to the conversation I was about to have.

"Are you finally coming back?" Harry asked. He knew most about why I'd left since I'd been staying in his cabin, but he didn't pry.

I frowned at the office door. *My* office door, and I nodded.

"I will be, yeah."

He grinned and patted me on the shoulder, "Good. It's been too quiet around here."

I didn't knock when I reached the office, just walked straight in. Ian's head snapped up and a scowl marred his features. His face blanked after a second, but I saw it.

"Blake," he acknowledged.

"You're done. This is my job and my station. You

were right, I needed to improve my performance but what you did wasn't about me. Months back, you admitted to me yourself that you'd clung on to your job in the team for too long before you applied for Captain. Now you're doing it again. You're too old, and you've already retired so it's not your place to make judgement calls around here anymore. I thought about it, and really, just fuck you," his mouth dropped and his chin hit his chest. "You came in here, threatened me, threatened my job and sat in that chair like you owned the joint. Leave. If you come back *at all*, I'll call the police. You want make falsified reports to your brother? Go ahead. The rest of the country's captains, the regulator, the police and the goddamn queen herself won't be able to get rid of me because I will fight you tooth and nail."

He sputtered, face turning a mottled shade of red, "You, you can't..."

"I can," I said firmly. "You know it, and I know it. Get out of my station, stay away from my guys and don't fuck around in other people's business until you've got the balls to back it up. You were my friend, Ian. More than that, you were my mentor. You really should work on this midlife crisis of yours before it starts bleeding into other aspects of your life too."

"It's not my life that's falling apart though, is it, Blake? Not exactly surprising that you couldn't manage to keep hold of that pretty little wife of yours," he leered.

A cold chill swept up my spine.

"How do you know anything about Carlie?"

His eyes were trying to portray a message that I couldn't read, but his words made me nauseous, "Poor lady, she just needed a shoulder to cry on, someone to support her in her time of need. She was all too ready to spill all her dirty little secrets when her husband's mentor popped round."

"You bastard," I croaked, fury ingrained in my voice. "I don't know what sick games you're playing, or even who the fuck you are, but stay away from my wife."

He strolled around the office, something so snake-like about the way he moved. Had he always been like that and I hadn't noticed? Leaning too close for comfort, he shot his parting blade, "She's not your wife anymore though is she? I've always fancied myself a younger woman. That little glimpse of her naked thighs and the curve of her ass on show in this office, it's etched in my mind."

He left before the words could sink in and it's a damn good job he did. Sick, sadistic Bastard.

I growled and punched out at the door, slamming it closed. I couldn't understand why he'd gone from being one of the best guys I'd ever met, to that monster. The only thing I could think of, was the job. He gave it up though, he retired, it isn't like I pushed him out. People have done worse things for less though I supposed.

The rest of the day passed in a blur of paperwork and banter with the guys. I couldn't figure out what Ian had been doing for three weeks, but whatever it was, it wasn't the job. Even the guys' hours hadn't been sent to payroll. It took me an hour or so to sort it out but I hoped they'd still get paid on time. A lot of them worked pay cheque to pay cheque, a delay would sting.

I met Zach at his house later that night and was greeted with the scent of garlic and steak as I walked through the door.

"Hey honey, I'm home!" I joked.

He appeared in the kitchen doorway, shaking his head.

"You've *really* got to start working on your sense of humour. If you expect me to greet you wearing a pinny and a cup of tea whilst asking you about your hard day at work, you picked the wrong guy."

"Do *any* guys greet people wearing a pinny and a cup of tea?"

"Ha! Don't ask me. Maybe someone with a weird fetish? Count me out either way!"

I grinned and brushed a kiss across his cheek.

"I made a decision today," I announced out of the blue. I was just as shocked as was when I finished. "I'm going to find a lawyer tomorrow and file for divorce."

"Wow, um, good?"

"Yeah," I nodded. "Yeah, it is good. I need to get ball rolling."

One of his eyebrows rose, "You could get more than one ball rolling you know?"

"And it's *me* who needs to work on my sense of humour?"

Before he could respond, there was a loud clatter from the kitchen and he spun around.

"Daisy, no!"

I followed him into the room and sucked my bottom lip into my mouth, biting down. If I laughed, his anger would switch from the dog to me and no thank you, she could keep it! The metal skillet lay on the floor surrounded by splatters of brown liquid. And Daisy? Daisy sat in the middle, wagging her tail, tongue lolling out to the side. Looking like she'd just eaten the best meal ever. I couldn't help it, I choked on a laugh and Zach growled.

Daisy barked and he snapped, "I wasn't talking to you. Get out!"

She whined, but skulked towards the back door.

"Should I, um, go and get the takeout menus?" I asked.

"No, I bought extra steaks in case I ruined them. Bloody good thing I did as well. Stupid dog."

"Is there a reason you're attempting to make dinner?" I enquired, knowing that cooking was not part of his repertoire.

He gave me a sheepish grin, "It's nothing special. Just smothered steak and chips. I just thought, well...I wanted to do something nice."

"Why do I feel like there's more to it than that?" I narrowed my eyes on him.

Looking away, he made an excellent job of studying the black and white kitchen tiles and slid his hand along the work surface.

"Well?" I prompted.

"I just want you to be comfortable here, Blake." His admission floored me.

"Why would I not be? If I wasn't happy here, Zach, I wouldn't be here. There's nowhere else I'd rather be. What *would* make uncomfortable, however, is a bout of food poisoning from your cooking!"

He snorted a laugh, "Dick. Even I can't fuck up with steak and chips."

At that exact moment, the smoke alarm started and blaring and Zack ran to the cooker. Smoke started billowing out as he opened the door and I had to hold onto to stomach, laughing so hard I could hardly hold myself up.

Struggling to breathe, I wheezed, "You were saying?"

He threw the tray of, what were supposed to be chips, but looked more like sticks of charcoal, onto the work surface, "Fuck this! I'm ordering pizza."

Still howling, I followed him into the lounge. He ordered food and an hour later we sat around, TV playing in the background, conversation muted as we munched on pizza.

I was adjusting to the normality. Part of me was still waiting for something to fall apart, but as the hours faded and evening creeped into night-time, I realised that was just something I would have to get over. Relationships weren't supposed to be built around drama. I don't know if I expected it to be different with Zach because he was a man, or just because everything had been so intense and we'd gone from zero to sixty in the space of a few months.

Either way, I had to get over it.

I wasn't going to live my life in fear of something going wrong.

Later that night, after getting into bed, getting jacked, sucked, reamed and fucking Zach so hard that I thought I was going to break him. I couldn't see. Couldn't think. Couldn't breathe.

His body covered every inch of mine and no matter how much I tried to fight it, I knew I would never be able to deny him a single thing.

He shifted away and collapsed, face down into the bed with a groan. I moved up beside him. Removing the condom, I tied it in a knot and threw it somewhere over the side of the bed.

Out of nowhere, Zach started to chuckle and within seconds his body was shaking with full on belly-laughter and I frowned over at him.

"I'm not sure if I should be insulted that you're laughing so hard seconds after I blow my load inside you."

Taking a few seconds to control himself, his body stayed still but his head turned to face me, "I was just thinking, do you realise that, granted it's still only been a short time, but this is the first time we've actually made it to a bed before you get inside me."

I thought back, "I've never thought about it to be honest. It's probably because we never had the time to! We're only just now allowed to have the time to play."

"Yeah, either that or because every time you get within three feet of my mouth, you want it wrapped around your cock!"

"That too," I agreed. "That mouth of yours should come with a warning."

Subtly shaking his head negatively, he held my eyes when he said, "Not much point in that anymore. It isn't like anyone else will ever find out."

Realising exactly what he meant, my heart thumped in my chest and I sucked in a breath through my nose.

"Yeah," I grunted, not wanting to show emotion.

He smiled.

I smiled.

He got up to clean up, I couldn't bothered, so I slept covered in me, covered in *him.*

CHAPTER
Twenty

I sat in the lawyer's office with my heart in my throat.

The pen shook in my grasp and my palms were sweating. Mr Reynolds, my lawyer, furrowed his brow at me over the rim of his glasses, probably wondering why I was hesitating. Like I hadn't already waited long enough.

It was just over three weeks since I had left Carlie, and I was finally ready to sign the divorce papers...or I thought I was. Doubts ran marathons in my mind. Was I doing the right thing? Would this drag on forever? Would she finally stop her incessant phone calls and texts? Was I ready to face the thought of everyone finding out about Zach?

I growled and threw the pen on the desk.

"Is there an issue, Mr Thomas? Would you like to delay?"

Running my hands through my hair, I paused to think. Zach's face filled my vision.

"No," I picked up the pen and signed my name without further thought. "It's done."

"Excellent," he smiled. Really? He seemed far too happy to be a divorce lawyer. "The papers will be filed this afternoon. These things can take time, of course. We'll expect the first response within five working days but in cases such as these, we just have to hope that the other party agrees to the terms."

'The other party' meaning my soon to be ex-wife. To me, it shouldn't have felt so clinical but what did I know? It's not like I made a habit of getting divorced, I wasn't well practised at these things. I couldn't fathom why she would have any problems with the terms laid out. The house was mine, the cars were mine and we didn't have any joint savings, kids or pets. The lawyer said she couldn't claim for the cars or the house because they were all in my name and I was the one who paid for everything, but I couldn't do that to Carlie.

The terms stipulated that I would sign-over the car that she drove into her name and although I wanted to keep the house, I would give her thirty nine thousand pounds - half the amount that had already been paid on the mortgage - to buy her out. Simple, precise and as far as I was concerned, more than fair.

It took three days for that thought to be shattered.

Zach and I had been out to a bar after I finished work, celebration drinks I guess you could say. Although that felt too harsh on my part, so we called it a date.

My first official date with a man.

My first official date with Zach.

We ordered drinks, snacked on bar food and just enjoyed the company.

I didn't feel the need to hide, didn't feel like I was being watched and I didn't feel like I was doing anything wrong. It was perfect and on the walk home, or the walk to *his* home, I told him so.

"Thank you, for tonight, I needed it."

He grinned, "You're too highly strung. You needed to relax and have fun. If sitting in a bar filled with greasy old men and drinking flat beers is your idea of fun, then I'm happy to do it with you."

"Most of those men were no older than me!"

He winked and bit his lip, "Like I said, greasy old men."

I slapped him on the back of the head and cursed at him.

I took a shower when we got back, threw on some old clothes and lay back on the sofa with an extended sigh. Then my phone rang...*again.*

Carlie had been ringing and texting constantly, pretty much since the second I left our home but I hadn't answered once. Two reasons. One, because I couldn't be bothered with listening to her complain and I wasn't interested in her mind games. Two, because she might cry. I didn't deal well with tears and regardless of anything else, the thought of her genuinely being upset, devastated even? No, I wasn't ready to deal with that.

I'd turned my phone off for a few days but since the divorce papers had been filed, I knew I couldn't avoid her anymore. I answered, but didn't get chance to speak.

"*You're divorcing me?!*" She screeched.

I held the phone away from my ear, "Carlie, I told you I was. This should not be a shock for you."

"I thought you were lying! I thought you were doing it for attention!"

I rolled my eyes. Fucking clueless.

"That's because that's what *you* would do, Carlie. I don't play games like that. If I wanted attention, I'd have asked for it. We're not together anymore and these last five weeks should have drilled that point home. Hell, the last six months should have told you all you needed to know! Just sign the papers, Carlie. We don't need to drag this out," I tried explaining, reasonably.

"Just sign the...*just sign the fucking papers?!* You're my husband, Blake. I can't just sign a piece of paper and be done with you!"

Actually, she could. I didn't say that though.

"Look, I'm not trying to be a prick, Carlie, but we're not in love with each other anymore. People don't stay married just for the sake of it," I paused to rethink that statement. "Or, at least *I* don't."

She sighed and then the line fell silent for a few seconds.

"Come home, Blake. Just...just come home, we'll talk. And if you still want me to sign the papers, then I will."

Goosebumps crawled across my skin. How could such an innocent statement sound so much like a threat? I felt the walls closing in and the gates locking behind me.

"I'm not sure that's a good idea, Carlie."

"Jesus, Blake! I'm not asking you to give me a kidney! I just want some time and I need to be able to understand this. Just a few hours, surely you can give me that?"

I let out a breath of air and could practically hear her grin.

"Tomorrow. I'll come round after work and we'll talk. I'm telling you now though, Carlie, I've signed the papers and I'm done. This isn't something that I'm going to change my mind on."

"Sure, Blake. See you tomorrow at seven," she

hung up.

I hadn't even noticed Zach come into the room until he spoke.

"That sounded like it went ok," he guessed incorrectly.

"Then it sounded wrong because she's toying with me."

I didn't tell him that I'd agreed to go and see her. It didn't seem relevant considering I wouldn't be there long and it was just a formality.

"I'm sorry," he muttered, causing me to shrug.

"It's not your fault, it would have happened eventually anyway," I thought for a minute. "Actually, forget that. It's completely your fault that this is happening. I'm so angry with you, I really think you owe me."

Catching my meaning, he grinned and rolled his eyes to the ceiling, "Really, Blake?"

I laughed and shook my head.

"No not really, I just want your mouth on me."

He stepped closer, leaning over me on the sofa and his lips brushed mine.

"You don't ever need to use cheesy lines on me. You want my mouth? You've got it. Any *time*, and any *place*. Yeah?"

I nodded my head slowly. My thoughts running wild with different ways I could take advantage of that fact. My manhood jumped, ready to be included in this game. Zach caught the movement and licked his lips.

"I'll give you my fingers, I'll suck you with my mouth and I'll drive you crazy, but this ends with you inside me. Ok?"

I jerked my head in some semblance of agreement. I wanted his fingers, I wanted his mouth,

I wanted us to drive *each other* crazy, but mostly, I wanted to feel the way his ass clenched around my cock and pushed me over the edge.

His mouth moved to my stomach and he lightly nipped at my skin before dipping his tongue into my navel. I shivered. The feel of his lips against my skin was...just nice. But I wanted him elsewhere and he was doing it on purpose. I snaked my fingers into his hair and pushed his head down. I felt his smile against my lower stomach as he went willingly.

"Get these shorts off me," I demanded, waiting for his hands to move to the waistline and lifted my hips. I kicked them somewhere over the other side of the room and pushed Zach's head back down.

"Suck me."

The wet, warm, heat of his mouth surrounded my cock, making me tug on his hair and push my hips up. He had one hand massaging my balls and the other on my chest, holding me down on the sofa. I felt the tip of his index finger creep towards my ass and I adjusted myself, giving him the access he wanted. The circular motions he made over my puckered hole were driving me insane, I wanted him to push inside.

"Stop fucking around and give me your fingers, Zach. I want it!"

He grinned around a mouthful of my cock, and pushed the tip of his finger inside, moving slowly until I felt the stretch and burn I wanted. Sucking deep, he pulled out and slid back in, letting me adjust to feel of him.

"Fuck. More, Zach. Give me more," I begged.

His mouth moved from my cock and his tongue sneaked out to lick a circle around my sack and then he sucked hard on my sensitive skin. My hips jerked and I bit out a curse. Moving lower, he parted my ass cheeks with his hands and his tongue dived in. He licked in tiny circles, driving me to the brink, then slid two fingers inside. His movements gained speed, pulsing in and out of my hole until I pleaded with him for more.

He jumped up and dashed across the room. Back within a second, he held a condom, a bottle of lube and he'd managed to ditch his clothes.

"I need you in me," he put one foot next to my hip, and straddled my thighs. "But this is about you. I'm going to ride your dick until you see stars and I feel the scorch of your cum in my ass. Lie there, watch me and feel me."

He sank down on my throbbing cock and I thrust my hips up to meet him.

"Fuck," I gasped. "You're so fucking tight."

I lay there, I watched and I felt.

I felt him everywhere.

His inner muscles stretching around me, his hands on my chest, his balls hitting my groin on his downward glide. He moved slowly until I could take no more, I took his hands in mine, held them beside us and grunted at him, "No more, Zach. Ride me like you mean it. Fuck me like you're searching for it."

He slammed down on my cock and my breath whooshed out of my lungs. Fucking *heaven*.

Tensing and flexing his thighs, he matched my upward thrusts, taking me deep and moaning his pleasure.

"Not going to last much longer," I warned him, feeling my balls start to tighten and my toes curl.

"I need..."

"Fuck, Zach! I'm going to come," I moaned, desperate for him to come with me.

He let go of my hand and gripped the base of his shaft, stroking himself. I reached down as he squeezed the swollen head of his cock and I gently clutched his balls in my palm. I stroked and fondled, reading his face for speed.

"Come on, Zach! Give it to me."

He shuddered, and I knew he was close. His tight hole squeezed my cock in a strangle-hold, milking every drop of cum from my balls. Through blurred vision, I watched him shout my name, cursing and moaning as his dick pulsed and creamy white liquid fell from his cock, coating my chest and stomach.

Still semi-hard, I flinched, groaning from the loss of heat as Zach lay forward and my shaft slipped free of his body. He sucked in a breath.

"Every time, Blake. Every. Single. Time. With you, it just gets better."

I nodded in agreement. Granted, I suppose I was still 'learning' but nothing had ever felt so good, "I love being inside you."

"I could tell," he joked. "One day, I'll be able to say the same."

I frowned, trying to work out what he meant. What my mind did the math, I swallowed.

"You...you want to...?"

His head came up, and wide eyes met mine. Raising up further on his arms, he stared at me.

"Of course. Don't you want that?" He asked, concerned.

Honestly? I hadn't thought about it, as ridiculous as that sounds. I loved his fingers, I loved his mouth but there was just something so powerful about the thought of having him inside me, inside the place that no one had ever been that scared me right down to my soul. He sensed it.

"You're nervous."

I shook my head, no.

"I'm not nervous, I'm petrified. It seems so, so…"

"Huge? New? Painful? It seems so what?"

"All of them. More though. There's no going back from that. I want you, I want to be with you, but what if this goes wrong, Zach? I'd be broken. For some reason, the thought of letting *that* happen and then ever losing you, just feels like something I couldn't recover from."

"That's…deep," he noted, and I nodded. "You'll get past that fear. I have you now and this doesn't have any choice but to work because we're going to make it. There's no giving you up now. Anyway, I'm not saying tomorrow, or even next week, but soon, I'm going to get you ready for me. I know how it feels and it's indescribable. I want to be the one to give that to you. I want to be the one who stretches you with his fingers, the one who licks your ass until you're begging for it. I want to be the one who opens that tight little hole wide enough to take me, who feels the inside of you pulsing and choking my cock. I want that. I crave it and you're going to give it to me."

My dick stretched, his words sending the blood from my brain rushing south. He smirked.

"You want it, you'll get it. Soon. But right now, we need to go clean up. We're going to go crusty if we don't clean this shit off soon!" He joked. "Shower with me?"

I shook my head, hoping he'd understand that I needed a few minutes by myself to take in everything he'd said and my reaction, "Do you mind if I take my own?"

"Of course not. You take the main bathroom, I'll

take the ensuite," he kissed me briefly. "I'll grab you a towel and meet you in bed."

He heaved himself up, and grinned down at me, "And Blake? Don't over think things ok?"

Easy for him to say.

CHAPTER
Twenty-One

"No," I spat. "I'm not going to keep going over this. Tell me one thing, Carlie. When it's written all over you that you don't really care either way, why are you fighting me on this? Just sign the papers and we can both move on with our lives."

It was not going well.

I woke up that morning, and headed into work dreading the visit with Carlie...and I was right to.

First, I walked through the door, she was wearing tiny little French knickers and a vest top - no bra - and she tried to kiss me. Second, she slapped me. Third, she cried. And finally, she'd taken to begging. I was *this close* to losing it altogether.

"There's nothing else to talk about," I sighed. "Either sign the papers, or we'll fight it out in court but the result is the same. I'm not coming back."

She fell to her knees in front of me, placing her hands on either thigh. I tensed.

I was sitting on the sofa with my legs spread and she had been pacing the room. Her being that close to me, having her hands so high on my thighs, it didn't feel right. The urge to escape roared through me. I tried to push her hands away and slide out from underneath her. She felt my movement and scrambled forward, straddled my lap and threw her arms around my neck.

My body turned to stone.

Sobbing, she pleaded with me.

"You can't do this to me, Blake. We love each other. We always have."

"You need to get off me. This isn't going to work," I picked her up by the hips, stood and put her back down on the sofa. "If you have nothing more to say, I'm going to get some more of my stuff and leave."

"You can't leave!" She cried. "Not yet anyway."

Her words made me pause in suspicion, "What's going on?"

Biting her nail nervously, she looked towards the front door and back to me, not answering. I had a really, really bad feeling. The doorbell rang.

"Just remember, I was trying to do something good. I didn't think you'd be like this. I just thought we could sort things out and now this isn't going to happen and I just thought...I thought...well that night was really good and you didn't mind the second time and we needed something good and...and..."

"Answer the fucking door, Carlie," I growled as the doorbell sounded again.

I didn't need to see who walked in. I could sense him. His voice, his scent. I couldn't avoid what was about to happen, so I stood with my feet apart, shoulders straight, arms crossed, and my chin held high. I didn't know how this was going to play out.

Zach walked in, followed by Carlie and he stood opposite me, mirroring my stance.

"What's going on?" He asked, directing his question at Carlie.

"Um," she stopped and bit her lip. "Well, you see, before, you said you were always willing to, you know, like..."

He sighed, she cringed, I growled.

Playing the part, I threw my hand out in their direction and laughed without humour.

"Are you fucking kidding me with this shit? *I'm divorcing you*, I actually filed the papers and you thought...what? What were you thinking, Carlie, because this shit makes *no* sense."

Her voice cracking, she leaned forward and screamed, *"You liked it! You fucked me harder the first night that he was here than you* ever *have before and I fucking loved it!"* she sucked in a breath and spoke lower. "You were different, both nights we had together. You wanted me more because he wanted me too. You'll see, Zach's cool, he'll do it again. That possessive side of you wants to come out to play."

She stepped forward and ran her hands up my chest to my shoulders, "Think about it, Blake. Remember how amazing it was, how hard we fucked. Remember how much it turned you on when you watched him lick my pussy and when his cock was inside me."

I clamped my lips together to hold back the vomit threatening to erupt and gently pushed her away from me. I remembered, and it was amazing. It was hot. It was beautiful.

At the time.

Now all I saw was Zach's face as Carlie sucked him, him throwing back his head in unadulterated pleasure. I saw his eyes on me. I saw him on his knees, sucking Carlie's essence from my dick and milking me dry. I heard the sounds he made as he swallowed and the way his throat worked.

I saw it *all*.

But he was *mine*.

His pleasure was because of *me.*

And I could have all of that without her there, which was exactly what I wanted.

Her desperate attempts at making me jealous had no effect. It was sly, part of me felt guilty because of the clouds of secrets in the room that she was completely unaware of. But what she'd done? It was completely unacceptable, crazy, and thoughtless. Completely Carlie.

"Jesus, you are actually insane," I whispered in shock.

"Um," Zach started. "I'm just going to go and let you two..."

"*No!*" Carlie shrieked. "You need to stay!"

"Carlie, honey, I never agreed to this. You said you needed to talk to me," he widened his eyes at me and I knew that he'd been thinking that she knew about us. "I'm thinking now is not a good time so..."

Ignoring him, she turned back to me, "You were *jealous*, Blake. Do you know what that means? You still love me, and I'll prove it."

She spun around, stalked across the room to Zach, leaned up on her tiptoes and crashed her mouth to his. I grunted, holding in my laugh. Zach eyes shot wide and his lips fused together as she licked along the seam of his mouth. His shoulders snapped back and his hands turns to fists at his sides.

Carlie pulled back with a frown, she was whispering, but I could hear every word.

"It's ok, Zach. You can kiss me. Trust me, it'll all work out nicely."

Eyes still wide as saucers, he shook his head back and forth. The poor guy looked terrified. I couldn't help it, I snorted, tried to cover it with a cough and failed.

Laser beams shot from Carlie's eyes.

"*This isn't fucking funny! I just kissed another man and you're supposed to be jealous!*"

The pitch of her voice slid through me and I shuddered. Enough was enough.

Quietly, but firmly, I asked her to look at me. She did.

"Would you look at yourself?" I started. "What happened to you? This isn't you, Carlie. I get it, ok? Do you think that when I married you, I wanted things to turn out like this? That I ever imagined they would? Not in a million years. I loved you, Carlie. So fucking much. I was proud to have you on my arm. I loved it that all the guys thought I was so lucky whenever they saw you at work functions. I used to smile when you'd get in a state because your hair wouldn't behave or because you couldn't find your favourite pair of shoes. But we grew up, darling. Or at least, I grew up. Nothing changed. You're still all about image. You care so much about what people think, what their opinion of you is. You've lost sight of who you are and I've lost the wife I loved. You know why we never had children, or why we never spoke about it? Because I was too wrapped up in my career, and you were too wrapped up in yourself."

"That's not true I..."

"It *is* true, Carlie. You're so obsessed with being perfect, how would you feel if your flawless skin was scarred with stretch marks? I can tell you, you'd drive yourself to distraction. I'm letting you go, honey. We don't work anymore because we're not made for each other. I can't pay you enough attention, and you can't understand my attachment to my job. If we were meant to be together, Carlie, those things would just be that. Things. For us, they define us. You're thirty-three, not some old spinster. You'll find someone else, you'll settle down again and be happy with who you are. Staying with me is making you crazy, and that's not fair to you, or to me. You need to spend some time by yourself. Find the old Carlie. Bring her back. When you find her, don't let her go because she was one of the best women I've ever met. As much as it hurts me, you're not my other half and I'm not yours. You need to find the person who owns the other half of your soul."

I fought to keep my eyes off the one person in the room who had taught me that. Carlie opened and closed her mouth a few times. Zach cleared his throat and pointed at the door, indicating that he was going to leave and I nodded.

Carlie's shoulders twitched as if she'd just realised he was still there and she looked over her shoulder at him. He closed his eyes as if in pain when he noticed the tears openly streaming down her face and I watched him flinch. Yeah, it was *not* a nice feeling. The lump in my throat grew thicker with every passing second.

"You're really leaving me?"

I slowly closed my eyes and let a single tear fall, "Yes, honey. We can't do this anymore."

"But...we love each other."

"Not anymore," I said gently. "You're holding on to thin air, Carlie."

She mouthed my words back me, testing them on her tongue. Her tears were flowing down her cheeks, little black streaks of mascara left behind in their path. She shook her head.

"You're wrong, Blake. I do love you. I always

have and I always will. You're my husband. When I said my vows to you, I meant them. To love and cherish, to have and to hold, for richer for poorer, in sickness and in health. I failed. Because I won't have you until death do us part. I can't look you in the face and tell you that I hope you find the other half of your soul, Blake. I can't do that and I don't think I ever will. You were mine to have, mine to keep. I don't know where we went wrong," she hiccuped in a breath. "I'm letting you go, too. Holding on is hurting me more than giving you up. I kissed another guy right in front of you and you laughed. Even if you still had the tiniest bit of love for me left, you never would have done that. I can't fight this battle on my own, Blake, and you gave up on me a long time ago."

I swallowed. Guilt, shame, heartache and pain flickered across my mind and made me jump forward. I grabbed her around the shoulders and squeezed her into me. Burying her face in my chest, she sobbed. I gave in and allowed the rest of my tears to fall.

Years ago, the old Carlie, the old Blake, they would have clung to each other in passion, in love and in laughter.

This wasn't that.

We were clinging to each other in agony, in loss and in goodbye.

I loosened my arms, framed her tear-stained face in my palms and whispered, "There she is."

She attempted a smile, but her face crumpled. I moved us to the sofa and sat, she curled up in my lap.

So I held her. I let her cry. I let her curse at me. I held her long after I needed to.

Hours and hours.

Long into the night, until the first streaks of sunlight kissed the sky and she fell asleep. Then I shifted out from underneath her. I lay her down and covered her with a blanket before kissing her forehead. I lingered longer than I needed to, longer than I should have. Her eyes blinked open and she tilted her chin up. My eyes fell to her parted lips.

And I kissed her.

Her tongue swept out, dancing with mine. Her fingers drove into my hair and I moved closer. I kissed her with all the love, passion and desire that we had lost.

"I'll always love you, Blake," she whispered against my mouth when we paused for breath, "But you need to go now."

I nodded, "Yeah, I have to go now."

"Estás rompiendo mi corazón, Blake. Pensé que tu eras mio para siempre. Salir, hacer lo que tienes que hacer. Te esperare por siempre si tengo hacerlo. Usted puede creer que su alma pertenece a otra, pero está la otra mina," she breathed, driving that blade deeper.

"I don't understand you, honey."

Her lips curled but her smile didn't reach her eyes, "You never did."

She turned her back to me and curled into the sofa, I took that as my cue to leave.

At the door, I heard her whisper, "Bye, Blake," but I couldn't turn to look at her when I replied, "Bye, Carlie."

Someone, somewhere was listening to Carrie Underwood and Brad Paisley's *Remind Me*, and not realising just how easy it was to forget.

Not me.

I had a feeling that song would break me. The

way my skin felt like sheet glass, it wouldn't take much to shatter me.

*You're breaking my heart, Blake. I thought you were my forever. Leave, do what you have to do. I'll wait for you, forever if I have to. You may believe that I don't own the other half of your soul, but you own mine.

CHAPTER
Twenty-Two

I found myself at the fire station.

Don't ask me how. Don't ask me why. I couldn't tell you.

When I left the house, I just knew that I couldn't go to Zach, and I couldn't be around people. So I found myself parking outside of the station, and I locked myself in the office.

I hurt *everywhere*. I had never expected that the end would feel so...final.

Realistically, I should have. I should have known how much it would hurt but I was too wrapped up fucking someone new, that I just didn't, fucking, think. And so I sat in the silence of my office, calling myself every name I could possibly come up with.

I admit it. I'm was selfish bastard, no, a selfish *cunt* and I couldn't take any of it back. In all the time I'd known her, I'd never seen or *felt* Carlie cry like that. She looked at me like I'd ripped her heart from her chest and stomped all over it.

I did that. I caused that pain. Only me.

I had to find a way to live with that guilt because right then, it was eating me alive.

Countless hours later, the guys had come into work and gone out on their jobs, without ever knowing that I was sat in the office. A knock sounded on my office door. I ignored it. It came again. Sighing, I stood from the desk and pulled open the door. With a sad smile, Zach walked by me.

"How did I know I'd find you here?"

I rubbed my face, "What are you doing here, Zach?"

"Rescuing you."

"I don't need rescuing. I need time alone," I said, meaning it.

Zach shook his head and leaned on the edge of the desk. He crossed one booted foot over the other and crossed his arms, "You need to forgive yourself, Blake."

He could say it, but it didn't make it true. He wasn't there at the end. He didn't hear her words, he didn't feel her tears. She wasn't his wife and he would never, could never, understand. In fact, him being there at all was just making me feel worse.

"Please, Zach. Just give me this. Let me hide, let me do whatever it is that I need to feel. I'm not doubting us and I know that realistically, I've done the right thing. I just need to, I don't know, hurt, for a while I guess."

"If that's what you really need, then ok, I'll go. I'll just say this. The pain isn't going to fade overnight, Blake. I'll be honest, I kept waiting for it to hit you but you seemed fine. Maybe you're just better at hiding it than I expected but I wish you'd let me there for you. It hurts me to see you like this."

I exploded, "Fucking hell! This isn't some romance novel shit, Zach! This is my life and it's my emotions. I can feel however I want to, for as long as it takes. *You hurt, I hurt.* That's bullshit. You didn't just leave your wife. You didn't hold her all night while she cried in your arms. And you didn't fucking literally *feel* her give up when you kissed her goodbye."

His head jerked.

"That's right. That's how much of a good fucking person I am. I'm with *you*, and I kissed *her*. Fuck! I'm as bad as those people you see on shit daytime TV programmes!"

"It was an intense situation, Blake. She's your wife, it's to expect I guess..."

"Don't you fucking dare make excuses for me. Yeah, it was intense and yeah, she's my *ex*-wife, but it doesn't make it ok. I cheated on her with you, and then I basically do the same the other way around. Who *does* that? I wanted to as well. I didn't even hesitate. Her mouth was just...right there and I thought about everything we'd ever done together and our wedding and the honeymoon. The way she used to wear her hair, the colour she painted her toenails. Fuck! I thought about her body and the way she used to laugh. I thought about everything in that split second and I didn't... fucking... *hesitate* to stick my tongue in her mouth."

"Jesus," Zach whispered. I winced, realising I hadn't meant to say that much. "Are you purposely *trying* to hurt me?"

I groaned and rubbed my hand down my face.

"No, of course not. I'm sorry. I'm so fucking sorry. I'm sorry I told you that, but I'm even more sorry that it happened. It was the last time though, Zach. I let her go, and she did the same. I think, I think...I think we were saying goodbye?"

"Why do I feel like a fool to believe you?"

I shrugged, "You're a lot of things, Zach, but a fool isn't one of them. I swear to you, I promise, never again. You hold the other half of my soul."

"Right," his lips twitched. "I held the other half of your soul yesterday too, didn't stop you kissing someone else. That's not going to mean you get away with everything. Just giving you prior warning of that."

I chuckled, rubbed the back of neck and glanced up at him. With a heavy sigh, I moved and leaned next to him on the desk.

"I don't want to be on my own," I admitted, watching him smile.

I meant right then, but when I said the words, I realised that I also meant ever. I didn't want to be without him, *ever*.

"I love you, Zach."

He didn't respond with words, he brought his hand up to my face, stroked the backs of his fingers across my jaw and leaned forward. He brushed his lips across mine, then pulled my bottom lip between his teeth. I growled.

"I win," he whispered. "I loved you before I even met you."

"I know," I returned, voice as low as his. "I just needed to catch up."

Our mouths collided and we moved together in a twisted rhythm of lips and tongue. He stole my breath and gave me his. My hand gripped the back of his head, anchoring him to me. I pulled away, sucking air into my lungs. His eyes didn't leave mine, his lips were still a whisper away from mine.

And the door opened.

My breath whooshed out and I scrambled away, standing and brushing down the creases in my shirt from Zach's hands.

"Ian," I spat. "I thought I told you not to come back here."

Zach looked between the two of us. Only his eyes moved, like he was frozen in place. His lips were puffy and pink, his eyes were glazed and filled with lust. If I looked anything like he did, my secret wouldn't be a secret for long.

Hiding his smirk, Ian stayed in the doorway, "I came to apologise for the way I spoke to you when I felt that you needed a break and the way I acted when you returned. I was wrong and I hope you accept my apology as a way of healing burnt bridges. I suppose that's it really, but I can see that you're *busy*. Maybe I'll shall see you around another time. I'll leave you to get back to your...um...meeting."

He turned and left without another word, but not before I saw the spoils of victory written all over his face. My legs started to shake uncontrollably. It was bad. Really bad.

"What just happened?" Zach asked, sounding worried.

"Life just happened," I sighed, "Fuck! He's going to tell Carlie. *Fuck!*"

Zach stayed silent while I fumed, until he didn't anymore.

"Um, Blake? Why is that so awful? She was always going to find out eventually."

"Yes! *Eventually!* Not two days after she receives the divorce papers and *definitely* not before they're even final. Fuck me, she's going to take everything from me, then kill me. She's actually going to kill me."

"Calm down, he didn't say anything. Maybe he didn't see. You don't know for sure that he'd even say anything anyway," Zach suggested.

I paced. Then I stopped and hoped. Then I paced some more.

"You don't get it! I'm addicted to you, Zach. *Addicted.* It's like nothing I've ever felt and even though the divorce is happening, I'm so consumed with guilt that I can't even close my eyes at night without seeing the potential aftermath of every move we make," I admitted. "I've never felt this full. *You* did that. You complete me in a way that I didn't even know existed. She'll see that when he tells her. And he *will* tell her. How do you think it's going to make her feel knowing that the guy *she* wanted for one night, I'm keeping him for a lifetime? Is she not already hurting enough? Will we ever be able to live normally? Or is this shit going to keep popping up again and again every time we get to a good place?"

"God!" He shouted, losing his patience. "You are so dramatic! Of course this stuff is going to come up right now, it's new! We're talking about a couple of days here. In a couple of weeks, it'll stop hitting you so hard and in a year, two, it'll be a thing of the past. Yes, you have reason to feel guilty, I'm not denying that. I do too. That does *not* mean that you don't deserve to be happy. So he tells her, it's not the end of the world. She might call you all the names under the sun and tell her friends what a bastard you are, but she'll get it out, and she'll get over it. Just like you will."

"I wish it was that simple," I moaned, knowing full well how petulant I sounded.

"It *is* that simple, Blake. What's done is done. There's nothing you can do about it. If anything comes of it, you just deal. Same next time, and the time after that, you just deal. Until the time comes when things just stop happening, and then you don't have to deal anymore. Most importantly, Blake. You are *not* going to have to do it on your own. Lean on me for fuck sake! You don't always have to carry everything on your own. You're such a..." he paused. "You're such a *man!*"

I stopped, stared at him, then I threw my head back and howled with laughter. When I could control it, I sucked in a breath and joked, "We've got real problems if you want me to be anything different."

"Oh yeah," he raised an eyebrow. "What's that? You not feeling being the woman in this relationship then, no?"

I cringed, "Don't even joke about it. I happen to want to keep my cock."

"Mmmm," he hummed. "Me too."

I tilted my head and studied him.

"How do you do that?"

"Do what?" He asked, confused.

"Every time I think the worst has happened, you just," I clicked my fingers. "And everything is all good again."

"Seeing as I'm usually directly involved in whatever sends you off on one, I'm going to go ahead and just say, it's a talent?"

Forgetting that the door was still wide open, I slid between his legs and held his chin in one hand, stroking my thumb back and forth over his stubble. I let my eyes move around his face, trying to figure out how to word what I wanted say. Nipping at his jaw with my teeth, my mouth kissed the lobe of his ear as I leaned in.

"No matter what, Zach. No matter what happens, no matter who does what, no matter if the entire fucking world is against us, I will never regret you. Not even for a second. I might overreact about things and be a miserable bastard at times, but I will never turn away from you. If it had been an hour, day or week, doesn't matter. You're the most important thing in the world to me."

He sucked in a shaky breath, "I'm a man," he croaked. "And we don't do this shit, right? But if we were allowed to, I would definitely be bawling like a little girl right now."

He laughed, "Look at us. We need to go home, crack open a beer, watch some football and bitch about women."

"In a minute," I whispered, my tongue sneaking out to lick his ear lobe. I smiled when a shiver ran through his body.

I inched towards his mouth, kissing along his jaw. Someone coughed behind me and I tensed.

"Umm, Bossman?" Matt.

I didn't move, but my eyes flew to the ceiling, "You have *got* to be fucking kidding me."

"What's up, Matt?" I asked, still not moving.

"Did you...um...err...did you know that you have an audience?"

My head whipped around and my hips and feet followed. Half my team, Matt, Marc, Harry and Dave stood just outside the office door. Their looks ranged from confused to downright humorous. I cleared my throat.

"Something I can help you with?" I raised an eyebrow, daring them to say something

"Yeah, who's the dude?" Harry asked, flicking his chin behind him.

Trust him to be the one who opened his mouth. I felt awkward. What could I say? My boyfriend? No. My partner? Definitely not. My soulmate? Oh yeah, I could just picture their reaction to that one. Instead, I stepped from between his legs and stumbled over his foot. I heard his grunt of laughter and flipped him off. The guys shared a chuckle and I rolled my eyes. Could it actually get any worse? I shouldn't tempt fate.

I tried to ignore the way Zach slyly moved his jacket in front of his erection. I did *not* need to be thinking about his cock in front of those guys.

Before I could answer, Matt spoke up, "Hey! You're that guy from the gym. He's the one who punched you, Dave."

For fuck sake! It got worse.

"Yeah. I figured that out for myself, thanks," Dave deadpanned.

Zach awkwardly scratched at the hair on the back of his head, "Err, yeah. Sorry about that. High pressure situation and all..."

He threw his hand out in my direction and I watched as it seemed to click in every one of their minds at once. Mouths dropped open, eyes bulged and one of them made a noise that sounded like 'whoa!'

"So you...and *he*...are like...?" I could see the wheels turning in Harry's mind. "You and he are like...he's your...for fuck sake, someone help me out here!"

I barked out a laugh, "He's my...my...he's my..."

I was no better at spelling it out than Harry was. I widened my eyes at Zach in a 'help me' gesture and he sunk his teeth into his bottom lip. My eyes fell into a scowl. A little help would have been nice. Instead, he just looked back at Harry and said, "Yep."

God help me, I was going to kill them all.

CHAPTER
Twenty-Three

Weirdly, the awkward situation at the fire station had made me feel better.

It wasn't life-altering news to the guys, it was just *news*. They hung around for ten minutes or so, shooting the shit with me and Zach, asking about the gym and nothing in particular. Then they left to start their shift, and that was that.

It felt...good. Felt nice.

It was a form of comfort, I suppose, to know that they had my back no matter what. And that maybe, just maybe, people wouldn't care. Or *most* people wouldn't care.

Lounging in Zach's bed, I flipped my phone over and over in my hands, planning out the next conversation I needed to have, listening to sounds of the shower running. I wasn't worried, my mum was a good woman and she wouldn't judge me. It was just the thought of actually saying it. Before I could think it over too much, I pushed the call button and put the phone to my ear. She answered on the second ring.

"Blake!" She cried. I rolled my eyes.

I was a shit son. I hadn't spoken to her in four or five months and she greeted me like I was still her angel. Yet another thing to feel guilty about.

"Hey mum."

"It's been so long! I was beginning to think you'd forgotten all about your old mum. You should talk to your mother more often," she chided, but it was light-hearted and she was just giving me shit.

"I know, mum. I'm sorry, I've just had some shit going on lately. I'll call more often...and you're not *that* old."

"Blake, language!" She scolded, then she laughed knowing everything I knew, I'd learnt from her. "Cheeky little shit, I'm not old at all, I just wanted you to confirm it. Should have known I wouldn't get it from you. So what did I do to deserve the honour of a phone call today?"

"I'm divorcing Carlie and I'm in a new relationship and I want you to meet him," I blurted.

The silence from the end of the line stretched on.

"Mum?"

"Sorry, sorry. That's, um, that's...are you happy?"

I smiled even though she couldn't see me, "Yeah mum, I've never been this happy."

Zach walked in as I spoke and I saw his eyes light. He sat close to me on the bed, still wrapped in just a towel. I surreptitiously watched the beads of water sliding down his chest.

"...it's shame but that's life I suppose."

"Sorry, what did you say? The, um, the phone line isn't great," I lied. Zach grinned.

"I said," she began again. "If you're happy then that's all that matters to me. It's a shame about Carlie, she was nice but that's life I suppose. Wait...did you say you want me to meet *him*?"

I looked to the ceiling, give me strength.

"Yeah mum," I admitted. "His name is Zach, he's

twenty-seven..."

Zach cleared his throat and mouthed 'twenty-eight'. I cringed, realising I'd missed his birthday when I left him. I mouthed sorry to him and his face creased as if he genuinely didn't care.

"I mean twenty-eight," I corrected, speaking into the phone. "You'll like him mum, I promise. He's a great guy and I just want you to give him a chance, ok?"

"Of course! You know me, Blake! If he makes my boy happy, then he makes me happy too. Are you coming to see me today? I'll put stew in the slow cooker now. I'll make dumplings too! You used to love my dumplings! Oh, I'm so excited to meet my boy's new *man*!"

"Mum..." I tried.

"Oh, Blake! Quick question before I have to go start the dinner. Now that you're enjoying life a little *differently* now," I cringed, knowing my mother and the fact that she was talking about my sex life. I did *not* need my mother talking about that. "Does that mean you'll finally agree to come and see that Queen Tribute band with me? They still play at the working men's club every second Saturday of the month."

"Not on your life, mum. It's never going to happen. Maybe you can ask Zach? He might like that sort of thing!" Zach's brow furrowed in confusion and I hid my grin.

"Oh! What a wonderful idea! We can bond over dancing to *'We Will Rock You'* and drinking cocktails!"

The image in my mind was a car crash waiting to happen. Poor Zach.

"Right, dinner at five. Later!"

The phone bleeped when she hung up.

I had just three hours to prepare myself for

dinner with my mother. That wasn't anywhere near enough time. I looked to Zach.

"Change of plans, we can't spend all day in bed. I can suck you if you're quick, but we we're having dinner at my mums at five and it'll take at least an hour to get there, more with traffic. I need time to tell you exactly what you're in for and to warn you that within five minutes of being there, she's going to ask you to go with her to see the Queen Tribute band that plays every second Saturday of the month at the working men's club that she frequents."

Zach eyes went wide.

"That's um, a lot to take in. We'll start with the blow-job. I can be quick. Sit up, put your feet on the floor," I did as he told me to and he dropped the towel, his cock already swelling. "Hold on to my thighs," I held on to his thighs. "Open your mouth. I want to fuck your face."

His pushed his dick past my parted lips and held my head still as he fucked my face. He hit the back of my throat over and over. I gagged and he pulled back, "Relax your throat and let it happen. I want you to take me deep."

I relaxed my throat, breathing through my nose and he pushed deep. I swallowed, taking his shaft even deeper. I felt him harden even more and stretch my limits.

"Grab your cock, Blake. Squeeze it hard, wank yourself, I want to see you come."

I grabbed my engorged cock, squeezed the base and squeezed, then I raised and lowered my fist, dragging my foreskin up and down. I was ready to come just from seeing the effect I was having on Zach. It wouldn't take long.

I reached up, fondling Zach's balls in my other

hand and furiously jacking my cock with the other. We were both reaching for it.

I hit first, groaning around his swollen member and causing vibration to shoot through him. His fingers dug into my scalp and he clawed at my hair as I drained myself dry with my own fist. Decorated with my cum, I moved both palms to the root of his cock and closed my hands around him, jerking him deeper into my throat and my eyes rolled back into my head when he rammed his hips forward and emptied himself into my mouth.

Taking a few minutes to recover, I shifted my thighs and stood from the bed. I plunged my tongue into Zach's mouth, kissing him with ferocious need and desire.

"Goddamn *wish* I had time to fuck you," I growled. "But we don't have that, so you need to go and put some clothes on before I have to phone my mother and explain why we're late."

His lips curled at the corners and I know he was as tempted as me, to cancel dinner with my mother altogether. He did, however, realise that probably wouldn't go down well and he moved to the wardrobe to get dressed.

It took another hour before we could leave and an hour and a half to reach her house, meaning when we pulled up on the driveway, my mum was looking out the window waiting for us. Her face lit up when she saw my car and she disappeared from the window, only to appear right beside me the second I stepped away from the vehicle.

"Blake! My boy," she held my cheek in her palm and whispered, "Gosh, you really *are* happy."

Overcome with emotion and feeling guilty for not spending enough time with her, I pulled her into my arms and buried my face in her hair.

"Yeah ma," I whispered. "I really am happy."

She squeezed me around the waist for a brief moment then looked up at me, "Let's go meet your new man!"

I grinned down at her.

Moving away, but keeping my arm around her, I held my hand out, "Mum, this is Zach. Zach, meet my mum, Mandy."

They shook hands, "Nice to meet you, Mandy."

Mum giggled and fluttered her hand in front of her face.

"I can see how you managed to turn this one's head," she hooked a thumb in my direction. "You're so...you're so..."

Zach cheeks turned pink and I laughed, "Ok, Mum. Leave the guy alone. You think he's hot, we get it."

During dinner, Mum did her usual talking too much thing and Zach seemed more than happy to let her. He didn't roll his eyes or balk at her. He didn't openly look at me to stop her from ranting. He didn't make excuses to move away from her. He just let her be, well...*her*.

It just made me think about the sort of person he was and the fact that I really didn't deserve his loyalty. But I had it and I'd keep it, forever.

I looked over at him, deep in conversation with my mum about the new boots she'd bought the day before. He didn't care about new boots, he wasn't that sort of guy, but he cared about them for her and in that moment, I fell in love with him a little bit more. He glanced over and saw me watching them so he winked in my direction.

Mum sighed mid-sentence and held her hand to

her heart.

Shocking me to the core, she whispered, "I'm so happy for you two."

Zach grinned, I frowned.

"Why?" I asked.

"Because this is rare and you're the lucky ones. You've found the other half of your soul. That's fate and its *magic*, Blake. Most people don't get to feel love like that for even a brief moment in their lifetime. It might have taken countless others on his part, and a marriage on yours, but you found each other while you're still young enough to have a lifetime of each other. *That* makes me so happy."

Speechless, I stared at her my mouth open.

It took a few minutes, but I recovered enough to ask, "How do you know there were countless others on Zach's part?"

She grinned, not looking a day over forty even though she was well into her fifties.

"Because, my boy, have you seen him? There's no way someone who looks like Zach could have kept all that to himself. Sharing is caring, Blake."

Ignoring her correct deductions of Zach's past, I moved on, "You really believe in that stuff?"

I had to ask, because she'd been single for the whole my life. Dates here and there, sometimes she'd see someone for a few weeks and then he'd vanish and she'd go on as if nothing happened. She didn't strike me as the kind of person to believe in soulmates.

"Of course!" She confirmed. "Blake, if you paid more attention to the world around you, you can see it and *feel* it everywhere. The world is full of love and affection, but soulmates are special. They stand out. They draw attention from others and it isn't for any other reason than they are the *definition* of happiness. It's in their faces, the way they carry themselves. Their aura bleeds reds and pinks, oranges and yellows. Right now, it's filling my house in a way that I've never had. I wish I could bottle it. Save it for the days that I'm alone and I want to remember. I never cared what job you did, Blake. Or where you lived, or how you spent your free time. I was happy to know that you were a good man who led a clean life. But this? This is beyond my wildest dreams for you and I'm so, so ecstatic that life gave you *this* man, to hold the other half of your soul."

I loved my mum.

She could be crazy, but she was the best woman I'd ever known and her words had floored me. I didn't want to ask, but I had to know.

"How can you still believe though, Mum? After dad...!" I trailed off when her look turned knowing.

"Your dad was, and still is, other than you, the best man I've ever met. He's charismatic and funny and he can make a woman weak in the knees with just one look. He's just not a man who stays. It's in his blood, Blake. I'm lucky that you got all *my* best traits and not his because I don't think I could handle two travelling men."

"Don't make excuses for him, Ma. I've seen the man about four times in my lifetime and two of those were walking past him in the street. He looks straight through me like he doesn't know who I am. I've come to terms with the fact that he doesn't give a fuck about me but I hate that you still care about him, Mum. He doesn't deserve to have that from you."

Biting her thumbnail, she glanced over and Zach and back to me, sighing heavily.

"He wouldn't acknowledge who you are Blake, because he doesn't know," she admitted.

"What?" I whispered, then stood and shoved my chair away. "*What?!*"

"Calm down, Blake," Zach said.

"Stay out of this," I snapped, losing my temper.

"Blake," Mum started. "He knows *of* you. He knows you're *mine*, but he doesn't know you're *his*. I couldn't do that to him, Blake! He doesn't know how to stay! That's why he ignores you, why he looks through you as if you're invisible. Because as far as he's concerned, you'll always be the reminder of the time the woman he loved had a baby with another man."

"But you didn't!" I yelled. "You didn't have a baby with another man! You had a baby with *him* and made me live for thirty-five years with the knowledge that I had a dad who couldn't give two fucks that I existed. God! That's...that's so fucked up, I don't even know what to say. There are no words to describe just how messed up in the head you actually are."

"Blake!" Zach snapped.

Hurt flashed across Mum's face before she shut it down. She breathed deep.

"I did what I needed to do to keep everyone in my life at the time happy. One day, you'll understand that sometimes it's best for secrets to follow you to the grave. I would never have forgiven myself if I'd have tied your dad down, knowing that for the rest of his life, he could never be truly happy, truly free. It would have affected all of us in the long run."

Unable to listen to anymore, I told Zach it was time to go and waited for him to nod before I turned and moved towards the front door.

I caught their whispered conversation before I left the house, "Don't worry, Mandy. I'll talk to him and he'll calm down eventually. Call me in a few days and we'll make plans. I'll take you to the Queen night."

I heard her, "Take care of my boy, Zach."

And his, "Always."

Before I slammed the front door, got in the car and punched the steering wheel. Zach joined me moments later. I drove in silence. Zach, sensing my mood, didn't even breathe loudly.

CHAPTER

Twenty-Four

I hadn't spoken in hours.

It felt like days.

My head was still spinning so fast that the dizziness made me feel sick.

But I couldn't break the cycle.

Zach was tiptoeing around me, weary of me. I *despised* that. The more he did it, the angrier it made me feel and the angrier I got, the more he behaved wearily. Swings and roundabouts.

Reaching boiling point, when he walked into the bedroom and asked me if I wanted him to order food whilst speaking like he was trying to tame a vicious dog, I just snapped.

"Jesus fucking Christ! Stop pussyfooting around me. I'm mad, angry, I'm confused and I have the urge to wring my mother's neck but I'm not some violent animal, Zach."

"Well, what do you expect me to do? Every time something throws you, you hide, leave, get angry or something else that I have no control over. You didn't hide and you didn't leave, so thank you very much for not understanding that I'm trying to help by staying out of your way and not getting up in your shit while you're trying to process something major that happened today!"

My shoulders slumped.

"I'm sorry. I'm just so...so *fucking* mad at her!"

He nodded in understanding, "I know and you're allowed to be. Be mad. Get it all out and then process. I told you. You just need to take the consequences and..."

"Just deal with it," I finished.

"Yeah. Deal with it. Whatever you need from me in the meantime, you've got it. Anything, Blake. Just ask and you've got it."

Thinking, I knew what I needed.

"Do you have punch bags at your gym?"

He grinned, "You bet. A boxing ring too. You feel like punching some shit?"

"Yeah," I nodded. "I really do."

We got changed and hit the gym within half an hour.

It felt good to attack the bags, to punch something that couldn't hit back. Sweat ran down my face and my back and my lungs were burning with exhaustion. It was exhilarating.

Zach didn't train. He watched. He stalked me with his eyes and I could feel the heat from his gaze from half a room away. People approached him to chat and he talked, but he didn't take his eyes from me. I think they must have gotten the hint pretty quickly because they never hung around long.

It felt good to have him there. Watching me. Wanting me.

It was also turning me on.

So I lowered my fists and turned to face him. He must have read the intent written all over my face because he too, turned and left the room. I stalked after him, following his footsteps until we reached his office and he forced the door open, pulling my t-shirt over my head and slamming me against the wall right next to the door.

My breath whooshed out and his tongue invade my mouth. Plundering. Twisting. Attacking.

There was nothing sweet or subtle about it.

He ravaged my mouth and I gave just as much.

I wanted to own him.

Someone knocked on the door.

"Ignore it," he gritted out, his voice low and gravelly.

The knock came again, "Zach!" Someone called. "You left your phone in reception, do you want it now or...?"

I moved to the side and he swung open the door, grabbed his phone and pushed it too again without a word.

His cock was straining against his joggers, begging for attention. Begging for *my* attention. I wanted him in my mouth, I wanted my fingers in his ass.

I wanted my tongue in his hole, his hands fisting my cock.

I wanted him on me and under me and bent over for me.

I was panting with fierce desire. The need to have him consuming me.

"I love you, Blake," he growled

Focusing on his mouth forming the words, knowing there was only one response, I replied, "I love you too."

He rushed at me, touching me from toes to forehead. Every bit of our bodies were smothered with each other. Desire burned through me.

"I want you everywhere," I grunted, tugged at his clothes.

"Everywhere?"

"Everywhere," I confirmed. My answer definite. I knew what he was asking.

He grabbed my shoulder and spun me around. My palms smacked against the cool office wall and I gasped.

"This isn't the right time. I'm too worked up, I need you too much, but you asked for it and I'm giving it to you."

I heard him suck. His fingers, I assumed. Then without warning, he pushed my joggers down just passed my ass and plunged two fingers into my hole. It ached, it burned but my cock throbbed and I begged for it. I wanted them deeper. I wanted another. I wanted *more*.

He scissored his fingers inside my ass, stretching me, preparing me and making my dick leak pre-cum against the wall.

"Stroke yourself," he whispered, so I did.

His fingers moved faster, fucking my ass with his hand and getting me ready to feel the length of his buried inside me.

"Your cock, Zach. Give it to me, I want it. I *need* it."

"I'm going to break you," he confessed. "I'm going to fuck you bare. You're going to feel every fucking inch of me and I'm going to fuck you raw. You'll feel the ache in your ass every time you move for *weeks* and you'll remember this."

He removed his fingers and replaced them with the head of his cock. He pushed in slowly, just the tip and my inner muscles burned. He was stretching me so wide, I started to doubt if I could take it. If I could take *him*. He didn't let me doubt for long. He pushed again, the smooth skin sliding inside me made me whimper and my forehead hit the wall in front of me.

"You'll remember it, Blake. For days, for weeks, for the rest of your life and you'll never be able to forget that *I* gave it you," he pushed again, still slowly, until half of him was buried. Then he thrust. I moaned, the pain combining with an overwhelming fullness to give me pleasure like I didn't know was possible. I thought I was going to crumble under the pressure.

He held his hand against my hip and pulled me back into him.

"Arch your back, stick your ass out," he breathed. "I want to watch you take all of me. You look so fucking sexy, Blake. Your ass is strangling my dick, I'm not going to last long."

He pulled out, almost to the head and I groaned at the sense of loss, of emptiness.

"You're going to want this every day. Every hour. Every minute. You won't be able to breathe free until you've had my cock buried to my balls in your ass," he plunged back in and my hand tightened to the point of pain on my dick, pre-cum leaked again, coating my fingers. "I'll give it to you. Every, fucking, day, Blake. I'll suck you, fuck you with my fingers, ream your ass with my tongue and I'll fuck this tight hole with my dick every...fucking...day until the day I die," he vowed.

His movements were becoming rapid, his rhythm faltering, I knew he was close but holding out for me.

"I want it, Zach. I want that. Your hand, your fingers, your mouth, your tongue and your cock. They're mine. I own them and I'll take them. Every. Fucking. Day," I broke off on a gasp as his shaft hit so deep, I could swear I felt the heat of him in my throat. "Fuck, Zach! I love you!"

"Fuck," he grunted, moving inside my body and pushing over the brink.

I stroked my cock as he pulsed inside me. I felt the warm, silkiness of his cum hit my inner walls as I spilled my seed onto the floor. He rested his head on my back, panting out his recovery.

He pulled out of me and I cursed. The burn returned, the ache throbbed but I missed him instantly. I felt his cum drip from my body and he groaned, watching.

"That is so fucking hot," he rasped.

My eyes moved to the door, noticing that he hadn't closed it fully.

"Jesus, Zack! The door's not closed properly! Anyone could have heard us."

He huffed, "Then they got one hell of a free show. We probably provided spank bank material for a year!"

I reached out to push it closed.

And the door smacked into my hand causing pain to splinter along my wrist and I cursed.

Zach eyes moved to the doorway and widened. His face blanched of all colour.

"This is...cute," Carlie said, standing in the doorway, voice carefully void of any emotion.

My whole body swung to face her. Without thought, I stood back from Zach and moved my hand to touch her. Her lip curled, she looked me up and down, taking a step back. I reached for something, *anything* that I could use to hide my still hard cock, whilst still moving towards her, scrambling to pull up my boxers.

She turned and ran.

"Carlie, stop!"

Still running, she screamed back, "Fuck you,

Blake! Just let me go! How can you even look me in the face, let alone ask me to stay and see *that*. I will never forgive you. Never. I should have believed Ian when he told me."

I fucking *knew* that rat bastard would say something. Even so, nothing, not a *single* other thing could have been worse than her walking in while my ass was still throbbing from the first time I'd ever taken a cock in my ass.

In her haste, she ran the wrong way, coming to a halt in front of the fire exit. As I neared, she crashed through the balcony door and stopped suddenly. I stayed back slightly, knowing she needed me away from her...also not knowing if she was going to throw her fist at me. The humid weather turned arctic when she looked at me. Her words were quiet, but determined and sure.

"I knew," she let out a self-deprecating fake chuckle. "Weeks, months, I'm not even sure how long, but I knew. I convinced myself that it was impossible. Just me being paranoid. My husband, the man who swore before God to spend his life with me, he wouldn't do it. He could never cheat on me *because he loves me too much.* I don't know if that makes me stupid or naive."

"You're not..." I started to interrupt.

"I know," she growled. "I'm not stupid. I'm not naive. This is all on *you*. What does it say about *you* that you would risk us, risk this, for a quick fuck with a *man*? Your wife, the woman who stood by and played second fiddle to your fucking job for the last eleven years, thrown away for, " she looked behind me and her lip curled. "...Him."

Knowing he was close, I whispered, "Please go back inside, Zach. Just give us a minute."

I winced at the pathetic thought that this could be fixed in a *minute*. This was irreparable. Having him around just wasn't going to help matters either way. He hesitated for a second, then said, "I know this doesn't help, Carlie, but still, I'm really sorry."

She launched forward and I put my arm out to stop her. Her weight hit me and I went back on a foot. Damn but the woman was strong when she wanted to be.

"Shit."

"*Fuck your stupid fucking apologies!* No it doesn't fucking help!" She screamed, fighting against my hold, but I refused to let go. "Does it make you feel good? Bet you think you're pretty fucking special right now, yeah? King Zachary fucking Black. Greedy *cunt* can't decide if he wants to fuck men or women so he *openly* fucks both. Got enough cock to share, right Zach? Big enough and bad enough to do whatever and *whoever* the fuck he wants."

She stepped out of my arms and moved back. Swiping her escaped tears with her hands and turning to face the street below, she asked, "Why not just shout it to world?"

"Free cock! It's decent, but not loyal!" She called, then looked back at me. "Make that *two* of them!"

I noticed an elderly lady frown up at us, but then, who wouldn't?

"Jesus Carlie, keep your voice down! Let's just go inside and talk about this," I suggested.

"I can *smell* him on you," she sneered at me, "I'm not going anywhere with you. You want to talk? Go ahead. Let's see..."

Oh fuck.

"Have you always been gay? Maybe I was just a ploy so you didn't have to tell the guys at the station.

It was awfully easy for you file for divorce. Makes sense now. Was it just too hard for you to keep hiding it when I brought a warm and willing *male* body into our bed? Or could it be that pussy just doesn't do it for you anymore? Maybe there's something special about sticking your cock into a tight fucking asshole. Is it the stubble? Smooth, soft skin just doesn't get the same reaction from you now?"

"Carlie," I edged forward but she stepped back again.

"Oh no, no way. You wanted to talk, I'm talking. Oh yes, we *both* know how talented that *cunt* can be with his tongue. What? I can't make you come as hard as he can? You like it a bit rougher?" She reached forward and gripped my cock in a tight fist. My breath caught in my throat and I sent a silent prayer to the skies to protect my manhood. "Squeeze a little tighter, suck a little harder, fuck a little faster? Is that it?"

I clenched my teeth together.

Never hit a woman. Never, never hit a woman.

"Carlie, that's enough, I know you're hurt but..." Carlie didn't let Zach finish, but she did let go.

Her eyes narrowed on him, "You stay out of this, you're nothing but scum. I know you're just trying to protect your latest fuck-toy but let's face it, you'll be done with him in a few weeks anyway. What difference does it really make if I break it now? Huh? It's not like I need it anymore."

She shook her head and closed her eyes as pain flashed across her face.

"It doesn't matter. None of it matters. You mean nothing to me. But Blake, we're done. I cannot and will not, *ever*, forgive you. I actually still thought you'd come back to me and I would have let you. I would have waited. How pathetic is that? You said once, though you probably won't remember, that you'd never let me leave you. Well, now, you don't have a choice."

"The papers are signed, Carlie. I already left. I'm sorry. More sorry than you can possibly imagine. I never wanted you to find out like this. This...I didn't do this to hurt you," I tried to explain, knowing that my words were meaningless to her.

She moved to walk around me to leave but I had to stop her, I grabbed for her hand. She threw her arms up and swung back, "Don't fucking touch me!"

"Vete a la mierda, coño. Haces mi piel arrastrarse. Voy a la ruina a usted, Blake. Su chico bueno reputación. Tu vida. Su carrera. Sobre," she spat. "¿Valió la pena, Blake? Su culo debe estar maldita puta especial. Más apretado que un monjas..."

Fuck you, cunt. You make my skin crawl. I'm going to ruin you, Blake. Your good guy reputation. Your life. Your career. Over. Was it worth it, Blake? His asshole must be damn fucking special. Tighter than a nun's...

Her feet shuffled backwards.

Zach called, "Carlie, be careful!"

I was too caught up in my own drama, too blind, too fucking selfish, to notice how close she was to the fire escape.

I could have stopped her.

I could have done something.

I could have done *anything.*

Too shocked, too scared, I stood in horror and watched as her heel caught in the metal grate at the top of the stairs and her face froze with fear. Her arms scrambled to catch herself.

Then, like she'd made a life-changing decision, peace swept over her features.

...And she let go.

THE END...
Of book one ;-)

<u>Book Two - The Only Man</u>
<u>available for pre-order on Amazon now</u>

<u>Book Three – HIM (The story from Zach's point of</u>
<u>view) will be available later in the year</u>

There is so much more to come from my two favourite boys in book two! I hope you get chance to finish their story with them.

HIM – the story from Zach's point of view, will not be a word-for-word replay of their story. For obvious reasons, there will be scenes the same but it is mainly a chance for you to get to know Zach a little more and give you an insight into his version of events.

ACKNOWLEDGEMENTS

From me, to you...

I am terrible at acknowledgements.
Each book, there are countless people who help me out with everything from cover design to promotions and I can never find the right words to say to explain how grateful I am.
I usually just end up offering my thanks in the form of sexual services! Quoting Annie Hughes – I have an endless amount of 'sex-debt'!
But this time, I'm going to give it a shot and actually try and use my words to say thank you.

Annie Hughes – 'Annie Hughes is my hero!'
Thank you Annie, from the bottom of my heart, for all the help you have given me with this book. Five hour phone calls, rants that go on for days, formatting, promotions, teasers & contacts...you've done it all for me. Meeting you has been the turning point with writing, for me because you've given me back the enjoyment that I had lost. The knowledge that you've gained from the industry in the short time that you've been writing has been invaluable to me and you are *officially* my soul sister. <3

Ewelina Rutyna – I haven't got around to offering you thanks in the form of sexual favours yet so this will have to suffice! Thank you so much for jumping in at the last minute and rescuing me with the edits for The Other Man. Your comments and changes were perfect and I wouldn't be hitting publish at all without you <3

Sarah-Jane 'Boobs' Bookham – I have no words. I sat for nearly an hour trying to think of the right thing to say for you and came up blank. You're the most helpful, amazing friend that a girl can ask for and I can't thank you enough for everything you've done for me. Your comments and suggestions for the story are so perfect and you never fail to come up with something special.
Thank you for always being, saying and doing everything I ever need and for keeping me sane when I was losing it. Love you Boobs <3

K T Fisher, Laura Barnard, A E Murphy, Kirsty-Anne Still and Amy Beth – You girls have become the support network that I never knew I needed. Each and every bit of advice that is passed around, helps in some way. I love each of you to the bottom of my soul and you all should know that whatever you need, whenever you need it, I'll help you if I can. (If you ever mention this in future, I'll deny I ever said it!) <3

Elisia Goodman (Dedicated Ink) – Thank you for all your support over the last year and for my amazing covers. Everyone loves the images you built and you should be incredibly proud of them.

And finally...**Bloggers**. All of you. Each and every single one. The job you do for nothing more than your love of reading is INCREDIBLE. A special thank you to all of you who have been involved in the promotions for The Other Man. I hope and pray that you enjoy Blake's story and you are looking forward to reading the next one to finish his journey with him <3

CONTACT ME
I don't bite...

Facebook:
https://www.facebook.com/daniellebreezeauthor

Facebook Page:
https://www.facebook.com/authordbreeze

Twitter:
https://www.twitter.com/authordbreeze

Instagram:
https://www.instagram.com/authordbreeze

Conversation is encouraged! My addiction to talking
feeds off your words ;-)

56516236R00140

Made in the USA
Charleston, SC
24 May 2016